Three Goo

Work, family, saving the NH

Geoff Lee

London League Publications Ltd

Three Good Years
Work, family, saving the NHS and Rugby League
© Geoff Lee

The moral right of Geoff Lee to be identified as the author has been asserted.

Cover design © Stephen McCarthy.

Photographs:
Front cover: The Dream © Arthur Critchley

A CIP catalogue record for this book is available from the British Library.

First published in Great Britain in August 2018 by:
London League Publications Ltd, P.O. Box 65784, London NW2 9NS

ISBN: 978-1909885-19-6

Cover design by: Stephen McCarthy Graphic Design
                               46, Clarence Road, London N15 5BB

Layout: Peter Lush

Printed and bound in Great Britain by Ashford Colour Press Ltd, Gosport, Hants PO13 0FW

About the Author

Geoff Lee was born in the Lancashire glass town of St Helens in September 1939 on the first full day of the Second World War, although it is believed that this was just a coincidence. His first experiences of the world of work were pea picking in the summer and potato picking in the autumn in fields around Eccleston and Rainford while he was still at school.

His real introduction to work was in 1957 when he became an apprentice with BICC (British Insulated Callenders' Cables) but known locally in Prescot as the Biggest Individual Collection of Comedians.

He began writing his first novel, which he originally called *Tales of a Northern Draughtsman* in 1988 a few weeks after he had started work in the CEGB Drawing Office at Harrogate. It took him eight years to write and then a further two years to find a publisher who changed the title to *One Winter.* This was because the novel was set during that terrible winter of 1962 to 1963.

This was followed by *One Spring* set in the early 1970s, *One Summer* set in the early 1980s, *One Autumn* set in 1992 and 1993 and *Two Seasons* set in 2002 and 2003. All his books have a general background of work, family life, old friends and rugby league, with the main character throughout the series being an electrical draughtsman just like Geoff was and all inspired by the old saying about being at work that "They could write a book about this place. It would be a best seller".

His latest novel *Three Good Years* is set between 2006 and 2008 against the general background of the world banking crisis and how the actions of the Blair and Brown New Labour Governments were affecting the general public.

He still enjoys listening to people talking on the bus and train, in the pub, at the match, or wherever else he goes and so frequently bases many of his story lines on what he hears from the public. He also draws material from what he finds on the internet and in various local libraries that he frequently visits.

He still enjoys meeting old school pals, work mates, friends and former neighbours and hearing what happened to them and telling them what happened to him since they were last in company together, sometimes well over 60 years ago now.

He also enjoys giving talks in libraries and once attracted an audience of nearly 40 people to Leigh Library, which so far, apart from now having had six novels published, and selling thousands of copies, is the pinnacle of his career as an author.

Thank You

London League Publications Ltd and Geoff Lee would like to thank Stephen McCarthy for designing the cover and the staff of Ashford Colour Press for printing the book. We would also like to thank one of Geoff's old school pals, Arthur Critchley, from up The Avenue for the photo of "The Dream" on the front cover.

The town of Ashurst is in south Lancashire.

Geoff Lee's previous novels about Ashurst, *One Winter, One Autumn* and *Two Seasons* are all available from London League Publications Ltd, www.llpshop.co.uk or can be ordered from any bookshop.

Contents

1. The Jehovah's Widnes

"Do you know what? In exactly two year's time, I'll be retired" said Cliff.

"You look tired now" said Colin.

"Well, I'm certainly tired of listening to you yapping all day long, that's for sure."

"So why did you come here with me today? You didn't have to."

"Well, I won't be here with you next Friday, I know that."

"Why?"

"I'm going back to that bottle works in Spain."

"Have you met a woman out there? This'll be the third time you've gone there this year."

They were both sitting in *The Volunteer* having their usual Friday lunchtime drink. It was something that Wilkinson's Drawing Office had been doing for years, although not always in the same pub.

"I won't be here next Friday either" said Tariq.

"Where are you sloping off to? Have they found some more mistakes on all them drawings you did on that Rabatext job?"

"No. I'm going to the dentist's."

Back in the 1970s, when around 8,000 people worked at Wilkinson's Engineering Works in Ashurst, the room would have been full, but today there were just eight members of the Drawing Office sat there. Now and again, an old work mate might turn up out of the blue and today it was Stan Middlehurst who had just walked in. It was the first time any of them had seen him for years because, after being made redundant in 1995, he had sold his house on Elephant Lane in Thatto Heath and gone to live on the south coast, in order to be near where his daughter Janet now lived.

"Hello Stan. What are you doing up here? Are you on your holidays?"

"He's always on his holidays, Cliff. He lives in Eastbourne, have you forgot?"

"Not any more, I don't."

"Don't give us some bad news, Stan. Don't tell us you are coming back to live up here."

"I am, but none of you lot need worry. My name won't be going on Ashurst's electrical register."

They waited while he took a drink from his glass and then he

1

explained why he had returned.

"My brother Jack died last week so I've come up to arrange the funeral, get the place tidied up, have the house painted and decorated and move in on Wednesday."

"That's a bit optimistic, isn't it Stan? It's Friday already, well it is up here."

"I don't mean next Wednesday. I mean on a Wednesday or a Thursday or even on a Friday. I'm not that bothered. I don't mind as long as it's not on a Saturday or a Sunday."

Typical Stan.

"So did you not like it down south, then?"

"I didn't like the fact that they had a dog next door that barked all day long, that all their bowling greens were flat, that the nearest pub was over a mile away and all their buses stopped running at bang on six o'clock."

"And what does your Janet think about you leaving? I thought that was why you went down there, so that you would be near to where she and her husband live."

"It seemed a good idea at first, Cliff. It would have been if she was like she was when she was still at school, but she's changed completely now."

"People do change when they leave home Stan, or when they get into their twenties."

"Maybe most people do change Cliff, but they don't all go and join the Jehovah's Witnesses."

"Oh dear."

"So where is this house that you are going to live in, Stan?"

"It's in Vincent Street at the back of St Helens Town Hall. My Mum and Dad, our Jack, Kitty and me all grew up there. I left when I got married. Kitty left when she got married and Jack just carried on living there on his own."

"Did he never get married?"

"No. He had a few women stay for their breakfast now and again, but little more than that."

"Is there still anybody living round there that you know?"

"No. Kitty was the last one and she died just before Christmas. When I first went down there, she used to ring me up about once a month. There were only three things she ever talked to me about though: how the Saints were doing, what was growing in her back yard and who had died.

2

The last time she spoke to me was to tell me that Alan Greenall had been killed in a bad accident on Mersey Street. A few weeks later she was in an accident herself and died soon after. I couldn't come up for the funeral as I had only just come out of hospital."

He took another drink from his glass, wiped his mouth with the back of his hand and went on: "I was really sorry to hear about 'Greeno', though I never agreed with any of his politics. He was far too left wing for me, but I always liked him as a workmate. How did his wife take it? She was Welsh wasn't she? I remember when she started in the Planning Office just before we had that terrible winter. 'Freckles' and 'Ban the Bomb' we used to call her. Nice enough sort of a lass, but she hardly ever spoke to anybody. Well, not until she started going out with him."

"Stan, I am very pleased to tell you that your Kitty got it wrong. There was an accident one Friday afternoon right after work. Alan was involved in it, but it was somebody else who died."

Stan looked in amazement as Cliff carried on: "Alan was stood on the pavement near to the gatehouse. A van approached with its indicator signalling it was going to turn left into the factory, but it didn't. It just carried on. Alan was just about to step onto the road when he was hit by a piece of wood sticking out of the van's window. It knocked him to the ground and he suffered some pretty bad bruising to his face and his ribs.

The gateman Frank saw it all happen, he rang 999, then came running out to see if he could help. It must have been the first time he had ever run anywhere for years. It was just too much for him. He had a heart attack and by the time the ambulance got them both to the hospital, he was dead."

"Well I am glad to hear that about 'Greeno'. So what has happened to him since then? Did he fully recover? Has he finished work now?"

"Not quite. He was on the club for a bit, then came back, with the intention of finishing work in September 2004 when he would have reached 65. But the week before the works shutdown, two electricians left at very short notice which meant that he had to go out and supervise a job at a cotton mill near Istanbul in Turkey."

Cliff burst out laughing and went on: "The conditions in the mill, and in the hotel that he was staying at, were pretty bad, to say the least. When he got back home, he said that, at his age, that would be the last time he was ever going out on site again. The following

3

day, our new boss Duffy told him that he wanted him to deal with an emergency that had cropped up literally that very morning.

Alan said he couldn't go because his passport had just run out. Duffy laughed and said: 'That's not a problem, Alan. You won't need your passport. It's only in the middle of Bolton.'

When he came back the next day and knowing how short-staffed we were, he told Duffy that he was prepared to stay on after he had turned 65, but only if he could work part-time and Duffy agreed. So now he describes himself as a part-time member of the international industrial proletariat or something like that. You know what he's like."

"Is he still a big union man, then?"

"We are all still in the union Stan, but it's not like it used to be when you were working here. I can even remember when we had over one hundred members. That was when Len Turner was the Office Committee chairman and when it was called DATA. I doubt if there are that many people working here now in the whole place, though to be fair, we don't have somebody like Basil Wilkinson in charge of it all and the conditions aren't too bad, considering."

"So where is he today then? He always liked to have a pint on a Friday lunch time, didn't he?"

"He doesn't work on a Friday now. He's probably gone out shopping in town with Thelma."

"And how is Thelma?"

"Fine. To see her, you would never think that she was turned 60. She works a couple of days a week in the Oxfam shop on Bridge Street, looks after the grandkids a heck of a lot and still watches the Saints whenever they are at home. She even goes away with them for some games."

"So how many of you still work in the Drawing Office, now?"

"In the Electrical Section there's me, Alan, Colin, Tariq, Jennifer and Shaun although we don't see very much of him these days. He's working on a big job at Drax Power Station, over in darkest Yorkshire."

"Is Jennifer the tracer?"

"We don't have tracers now, Stan. They went a long time ago. She's something of an expert on Tariff Metering and Meter Compensation Calculations and pretty good on CAD as well."

"Do you think I could get my old job back in there with you?"

"Stan, if we want one of your brackets drawn now, all we have

4

to do is press a few buttons on a computer and it's done in five minutes."

"I guessed you would say summat like that."

"So how are you going to spend all your time, once you are living back up here, Stan?"

"The first thing I am going to start doing again is bowling and by that I mean crown green bowling."

"Obviously."

"The second thing I'm going to start doing again is watching the Saints and when I've got myself all sorted out, I am going to start writing a novel."

"You writing a novel. What about?"

"When I was down there, I started looking into our family tree. There was not very much else interesting for me to do. I was amazed at some of the things my uncle Norman did when he lived in Widnes. So I decided that I could write a novel based on him and the weird disappearance of his second wife."

"What are you going to call it, Stan?"

"I don't know yet, although bearing in mind what our Janet and uncle Norman have done between them, I might just call it 'The Jehovah's Widnes'."

"Do you think they might give it a review in *The Watchtower*?"

"They won't. Not after they have read the first page."

"Why, what's on it?"

"It's something that Napoleon once said."

"What?"

"Glory is fleeting. Obscurity is forever."

"Were you ever religious, Stan?"

"Well, I used to go to Sunday school every week until I was just turned 16. That was when a few of us decided to form a football team and play on the church field in the Under-19s League. The Vicar agreed to us doing that, as long as whoever played for us came to our church, at least once a month.

That was no problem until we signed a lad from Park Rangers. He was a centre forward and a good 'un too. In fact a couple of years later he played a few games for Tranmere Rovers. The only trouble with him was that he was a Roman Catholic which meant that he couldn't come to a Church of England church. When the vicar found out, he said that if he ever played for us again, we could all go and play on somebody else's field.

Luckily for us, the dad of one of our team worked at Grange Brewery. They had their social club then, down Ashton Lane and with a pitch they only played on every other Saturday in the Open Age League. So we moved in with them, changed our name to Grange Dynamo and except for going to a few funerals and the odd wedding or four, I haven't been inside a church since."

Soon it was time for them all to return to work. They took their leave of Stan, who was now going to visit his solicitor just to make sure that his recently departed brother hadn't left the house and all his money to some Home for Lonely Dogs.

Back in the Drawing Office a few minutes later, they were quite surprised to see Alan sat there in front of his computer. Their boss Duffy had rung him an hour earlier, wanting to talk to him about an order that the Amsterdam office were in the process of negotiating. It was quite a complicated order, one that would require Alan's immediate advice and attention.

Soon after, he went to see their boss and returned just before finishing time, with the news that most of them would be spending the next few weeks, designing equipment for a chemical plant based at Dole, a small town in eastern France.

Then Alan asked them what had happened in the pub at lunch time. He was pleased to hear that his old pal Stan was coming back up north and going to start watching the Saints again. Alan had some good memories of Vincent Street and particularly at one house right at the far end, the scene of some pretty wild parties in the early 1960s: well, wild by Gerard's Bridge standards!

They all walked out of the office together, with everybody except Alan, heading for the work's car park. A few minutes later he was stood close to the spot where his accident had taken place, now nearly three years ago, waiting for Thelma to pick him up. He made a point of standing well back from the kerb though, just in case there was a repeat of what had happened there before.

Three cars slowed down as they approached him, with each driver winding the window down and shouting out to him:

"Do you want a lift, Alan?"

Finally, Thelma drove up rather slowly and greeted him with the news that she thought that there was something wrong with the clutch.

"That settles it then."

"What?"

"We'll have to go in Phil's car."

Phil was their next door neighbour and their journey that evening, would be to Knowsley Road to watch the Saints play their local rivals from Warrington. It would be a bit of a coincidence Alan thought, if he were to see Stan stood there on the terraces.

Ignoring the fact that he might have to find time to look at the clutch, the day had clearly been a good start to the weekend. On Saturday, he would be spending the afternoon in Gillarsfield Conservative Club on Makerfield Road. Well, not in it, but on its bowling green, playing for Southport Edge Miners' Welfare in the Ashurst Crown Green League Division Two. Despite its name though, none of the team had been underground for over 20 years, and in Alan's case, never.

On Saturday evening, their son Robert and his partner Megan were coming round for a meal to celebrate Robert's birthday. That would almost certainly mean that quite a large amount of alcohol would be drunk. He also knew that if he was going to have full control of this job at the chemical plant at Dole, there would almost certainly be a need for him to make at least one site visit, two if he thought that could get away with it! And if that did happen, no doubt he might be able to arrange for a little trip across the border into Switzerland over the weekend.

Then he thought to himself how lucky he had been in his whole life, never having been sacked, or made redundant. Unlike most of his mates, right across Merseyside and South Lancashire, he had never even been on the dole and now he was going to spend time working at Dole. Funny old world!

2. Minnie Cotton versus Dewsbury

"What are you wearing tonight?"

It was the question Alan usually asked Thelma while they were eating their evening meal before going to watch the Saints.

"My Vollenhoven top. I washed it yesterday."

"Is it dry?"

"No, it's wringing, soaping, sopping wet. It's still in the washing machine."

Typical Thelma.

"Have you seen the team?"

"Yes, I saw one of the under–19s buying something for the weekend in Wainwright's chemist's this afternoon and a bit later on, I saw Keiron waiting for a bus outside the Nags Head."

She was clearly in fine fettle, but then she always was, whenever she knew that they would soon be going to the match.

"Have you told Phil that we'll have to go in his car?"

"Yes. He said that he'll be round in about half an hour."

Ten minutes later there was a loud knock on the front door.

"Phil's early" said Thelma as she went to answer it.

But when she opened the door, it wasn't their next door neighbour Phil who was stood there. It was a middle aged couple, both decked out in primrose and blue, the colours of tonight's opponents from a few miles down the road.

The woman spoke a little nervously: "Hello, Mrs Greenall I don't think that we have met before, but we are your new neighbours. We have just moved in over the road at number five."

"Pleased to meet you. I'm Thelma."

"Yes, we know your name. Mr Reynolds told us."

"So what can I do for you both?"

"We were hoping to go to the match tonight, but our car won't start. Is there any chance we could come with you? It was Mr Reynolds who told us you would be going in your car. You usually do, he said."

"Well you can't come in our car. The clutch has packed in and we are having to go in our next door neighbour's car."

Her face fell until Thelma went on to say she was sure they could all squeeze into it.

"Come in and meet my other half while I go and ask him."

8

A couple of minutes she was back.

"No problem as long as you two don't mind travelling, hidden under a blanket in the boot!"

By the time they reached the ground Thelma had discovered some interesting things about their new neighbours. Margery had once lived in Swansea, a town not that far from Tonyrefail where Thelma had spent the first year of her life. She had a keen interest in gardening and used to work at the Alder Hey Children's Hospital in Liverpool. She talked a lot, not like her husband Cyril who did not say much all the way to the ground. He said even less on the way back, as the Saints won comfortably 34–22.

Later Alan discovered that Cyril had grown up in Penketh, on the outskirts of Warrington, and used to work in the Accessories Division of British Insulated Callenders Cables at Prescot until it had been closed down over 10 years ago now. Cyril also knew Alan's old pal, John Rigby who had then lived in a house close to the Prescot Cables football ground in Hope Street.

'Riggers', had also worked in the Accessories Division at the BI before coming to Wilkinson's in 1972. However, Cyril knew nothing about what had happened later to him or his band, *The Rainmen*, so called because two of their group came from Rainhill and one came from Rainford.

As they drove along Boundary Road it looked as though there was going to be a big crowd, but Phil still managed to squeeze his car into a space in Doulton Street. As they set off for the short walk to the ground, Margery said: "We are going to meet Cyril's brother and his wife behind the sticks at the Eccleston end. Can we still come back with you?"

"As long as Saints don't lose" laughed Phil.

They were soon standing in their usual spot on the halfway line. Alan looked round to see who was there. As usual, most of the regulars were stood dotted around. Three of them used to work on the shop floor at Wilkinson's, another was the son of Mr and Mrs Astbury who had once been their neighbours in Chisnall Avenue where Alan had grown up with his mother, sister Joan and brother Paul. Two guys he often saw there came from Leeds for every home game. They had always followed Saints, though for what particular reason Alan did not know although some time later he found out why, in some rather unusual circumstances.

Not far away he saw 'Little and Large', so called because one was over six foot two and the other was not much taller than Thelma. Large always had a very good view of what was happening on the pitch, but Little didn't and was forever saying to his mate "What's happened? What's happened?"

One person who Alan hadn't seen for a long time was 'Move Up'. He was called that because nearly every time an opposing player was getting up to play the ball, he would shout out loudly: "Move up, Saints, move up" and often, with his arm, he would indicate the direction in which they had to move. Where was he now, Alan wondered? Maybe with the passage of time he had moved up in society and was now sitting in the stand.

Not far away he could see a lady from Haydock, someone who had a vocabulary that would have shocked a bin man or bottle hand. He remembered clearly one match when he had been stood near her and had heard a spectator ask her how much she had paid to get in. When she told him, he replied that she had paid far too much. She should have paid only half what she had done, because she only ever watched one side.

"A bit like all the referees that come here from Chapeltown Road then." was her reply.

Another fan who Alan knew quite well was Minnie Cotton. In 1966, he was at Swinton watching the Saints playing Dewsbury in the Challenge Cup semi-final when she had made national headlines. At the time, her lodger was the Saints second-row forward, the Welshman John Warlow. During the second half and with the Saints losing, John had come in for some pretty rough treatment from members of the opposing pack. It had happened close to where Minnie was sat on the edge of the pitch. Incensed by what she had seen, but which neither the referee nor the touch judges had acted on, she had dashed on to the pitch, armed with the umbrella of the woman sat next to her, and which she used to beat the living daylights of whoever was playing for the Yorkshire side. It didn't take long though before she was escorted off the field by a police superintendent and into rugby league folklore.

He recalled another big game, this time against Huddersfield, four years earlier, when the Saints South African winger Tom van Vollenhoven had been flattened by a vicious stiff arm tackle. Alan remembered seeing him lying on the ground with blood streaming from his nose on to the snow. Then the referee, 'Sergeant Major' Eric Clay called the offending Huddersfield player over to him. Next

10

to appear on the scene was Alex Murphy, keen as ever to give his advice. Whatever he said did not please Mr Clay, who promptly sent the pair of them off the field.

A woman who was stood near Alan was clearly incensed by this decision. She was beside herself with rage, pushed her way to the front and tried to climb over the wall to get at Mr Clay. She was quite a well-proportioned lady, but failed three times to do so. Nobody said anything to her. In that situation, no matter what they might have said, she would clearly have clocked them one.

On leaving the ground he had walked up Dunriding Lane to catch the bus into town. Outside the Bird I' th Hand pub, there were many Huddersfield fans all stood around a dozen coaches parked nearby and right in the middle of this very happy crowd of Yorkshire folk, he saw her again, wanting to take them all on.

As he stood there, listening to Thelma talking to her friend, Brenda from Haresfinch, Alan remembered how different things were when he had first started watching the Saints. Then, he had watched the game, stood in the boys' pen with all his mates from school. There was no music in those days because there was no tannoy and any changes to the team that was printed in the programme, were chalked on a board that a boy carried round the pitch a few minutes before the kick-off. If it was a really big game, a brass band might have performed before a very appreciative audience. Otherwise all the noise came from around 20,000 to 30,000 people chattering away loudly to each other.

Things were so different now he thought, but then he was approaching the age of 67 and the magic of seeing his heroes was not like it used to be. Many of the players that he now watched were young enough to be his grandchildren. It was just not the same, but then he knew how lucky he was, to have been a rugby league fan for most of his life. It wasn't only watching the entertainment on the field, either. It was like being a member of a large family. Yes, there was great rivalry on the field, but away from the ground, there was also great friendship something that he had experienced for as long as he could remember.

There was all the humour associated with the game too and the tales told by players and spectators alike, about what used to happen, both on and off the field. Like the time the Saints were playing Whitehaven and one of their team had complained to the referee that a Saints player had bitten him. He showed the referee

11

his arm and then pointed to the Saints hooker, the Irishman Tom McKinney. The referee immediately sent him off. Tom said it wasn't him that had done it, but the referee was having none of it so Tom, opened his mouth to reveal that he didn't have any teeth, something that had happened during the last 10 years that he had spent playing the game!

Then there was the time he heard Ray French being interviewed on Radio Merseyside. It was about Ray's first Good Friday game and he recounted how he was sat in the dressing room preparing for his first Wigan derby and feeling a little nervous. He looked up and saw Alex Murphy looking in front of a mirror on the wall, carefully putting Brylcream on his hair and then combing it. Ray asked Alex whatever was he doing with less than 10 minutes to go before kick-off.

Alex's reply was classic: "Ray, just your mam and dad have come to watch you. There's nearly 29,000 out there that have come to watch me."

At the next meeting of these two great local rivals, as the teams were coming out of the dressing rooms at Central Park, the burly Wigan no nonsense, heavily built, prop forward John Barton had nodded to Ray, pointed at him and said loudly: "I'll see you after the game."

"Have you upset him already, Ray?" asked one of his team mates as they ran out on to the pitch.

"No. He's got some tomato plants for me."

At this point, the Warrington team came out of the tunnel to a great roar from their large group of supporters, all standing together at the Eccleston end of the ground and now including their new neighbours, Margery and Cyril.

By half-time though, the game looked over and done with, because the Saints went into the dressing rooms winning 26–4. But a great rally by the visitors reduced the arrears to two points until an interception and a 70 metre dash to the line in the last few minutes by the Saints winger Ade Gardner ensured a home victory. Many said his try was reminiscent of the winger Tom van Vollenhoven, few of them though, unaware that their former favourite was over from South Africa and was sat in the stand with all the directors, watching the game.

Back home a few hours later, they were sat chatting about the game, what Brenda had told Thelma about her son Tommy who had just emigrated to Australia and then their new neighbours.

12

"I took a liking to Margery straight away" Thelma said.

"I think they'll be a welcome addition to our street, though I hope they don't have too much trouble with their next door neighbours."

At number three in Silkstone Street lived the Tyrer family. Sometimes it was just Mr and Mrs Tyrer and their two dogs who were there. Sometimes though, one, two or three of their children lived there as well. Not all the time though because from time to time, they would be found lodging at Her Majesty's pleasure. Currently all three of them had addresses at either Walton in Liverpool or Strangeways in Manchester and the earliest the first of them would be let out would be March 2008.

It was rather strange Thelma making that statement about the Tyrers then, because the following morning, as she opened the curtains in the front room, she saw a police car parked outside the Tyrer's house. Later she heard from a neighbour that Mrs Tyrer had been arrested for her involvement in some rather stupid online computer fraud.

A few days later the two dogs were taken away in a van by a man wearing a white uniform and soon after, the house was put up for sale. Soon after, Thelma was shopping in ASDA when she bumped into Margery: "I don't know what you and your Cyril did to the Tyrers, but whatever it was, it worked. Let's just hope whoever buys their house next, are as nice as you two are."

"Well if it's the young couple who were round again last night I'm sure they will be, Thelma."

"Have they got any dogs?"

"I don't think they have. But I do know that they have got three young children, so we'll just have to wait and see."

"Or maybe you'll just have to wait and then listen to them."

3. Lord Beeching has been beaten before

"Did you go to the match on Friday night, Jennifer?"

"Yes".

"Did you enjoy the match on Friday night, Jennifer?"

Silence.

"I take it that's a no."

It was Monday morning, and a good time for any Saints fans in the factory to have a go at any Warrington fans who worked there, following Friday night's game.

"Did your Mary go with you?"

"Yes."

"And did she enjoy it?"

"Yes. She was a bit quiet at first, but by half-time she was cheering, although she must have been the only person in the ground to be cheering players from both sides. She kept asking me what was happening and why the referee had blown his whistle. But by the end of the game she seemed to have grasped all the basics."

Jennifer had joined the company after graduating with a degree in Electrical Engineering at Salford University. As a child she had grown up in County Durham and among her early childhood memories were those associated with the 1984 to 1985 miners' strike and seeing her cousin Dave and uncle Jimmy being roughly treated and then arrested by four policemen. She had never forgotten the events associated with that bitter struggle and had helped shaped her general outlook on life ever since.

She had an older sister called Mary, but she was only older by about five minutes. She had also gone to university although in her case it was the London School of Economics. On graduating, she had worked in a stockbroker's office in the City, but after a few months there, had moved to New York where she spent a year working on Wall Street. On her return to England she had spent time in a bank followed by the last three months working for an insurance company. She now lived with her boyfriend who was a trader on the Stock Exchange, all of which explained how she knew so much about the inner workings of the financial world.

Sometime after they had both left university, their father, a Quality Control inspector, had lost his job in Sunderland, but luckily had soon found another. However that had meant that he and their mother had to leave the North East and move to Bryn in Wigan because his new place of employment was at the nearby Heinz factory at Kitt Green. This was the reason why Jennifer was now living with her parents again and able to travel the short distance to work on the bus each day.

Although the two worked in totally different environments, they shared many views about life in general and particularly about the distribution of the country's wealth. What had finally convinced them both that they could no longer sit back and watch the situation in the country worsen, was the Labour Government's illegal invasion of Iraq in March 2003.

Mary had never had much time for New Labour, unlike Jennifer who had once been quite impressed by Tony Blair. But as the party that she was at one point considering joining, had continued to carry out its neo liberal free market economic programme, she had changed her mind. Now she had little time for nearly all of its MPs except maybe for Dennis Skinner, Michael Meacher, Jeremy Corbyn and little more than a dozen or so others.

Soon after, the two of them decided to set up an organisation whose main aim would be to campaign against the growing shift of the nation's wealth into the hands of a very small percentage of the population. At first there were only eight of them in their group and, except for Mary, they all lived in the area around Ashton, Billinge and Bryn.

Mary kept in regular contact by e-mail, telling them about what was happening in the financial world and regularly circulating drafts of articles for a magazine that they had decided to produce and which they called *The Gap*. When Jennifer had mentioned what she was beginning to get involved in, to Alan and all the other draughtsmen, she had expected that they all would start making jokes about what might go on page three and whether it would include a lonely hearts column, a crossword and the football results.

She was very pleased though at the response that had been shown in particular by Alan, Cliff and Tariq. Alan had even written an article for the second issue. It did not have anything to do with the distribution of the country's wealth then, but described how Lord Beeching had been prevented from closing Ashurst railway station in 1962. It was a well written piece, mainly because Alan had been very active in that campaign. When he read it, Cliff remembered a similar campaign around the same time had prevented Lord Beeching closing the line that ran from Wigan North Western, through Bryn, Garswood, St Helens Shaw Street, Thatto Heath, Eccleston Park, Prescot and on to Huyton and then Lime Street. That was because his brother had been heavily involved in that campaign too, although sadly he had recently passed away.

After Thelma had read the first issue, she had offered to take a few copies to sell to her friends and to people that she had got to know through working in the Oxfam shop on Bridge Street. There she regularly met a regular stream of people, all with tales to tell about how bringing up a family was becoming more and more difficult. One of them had once been a Labour councillor but she had resigned, in disgust with some things said or done by a couple of the party's top brass in London.

Other members of their group included a single parent from Gillarsfield, whose father used to work at the Anchor Cable Works in Leigh, Maria, now in her last year at school, and aiming to go to university and Scottish Margaret. She came from Aberdeen and had become friends with Jennifer when they were both at Salford University. Her sympathies lay a little more with the SNP, but that did not stop her having plenty in common with the rest of the group. This included Mark. who worked as a teacher at Ashurst Comprehensive, Gerald who lived in the same street as Jennifer and used to work at Billinge Hospital and Tommy, a postman who had played for three seasons with Hemsley Hornets.

Mary rarely attended any of their meetings, but still liaised with them, mainly through long telephone conversations with Jennifer. She also had a good friend who held an important position in the Civil Service, and so had to remain anonymous. She was the source of much useful information about how various members of the Establishment operated. In this way, they all began to learn much about the inner workings of the finance industry, how so much wealth there was in the world, and how it was so unfairly held in the hands of such a small number of the world's population, with most of them based in North America.

Lunchtime at work had always been a good time for interesting conversations. Sometimes it would be sparked off by what had been on the News the previous night. Sometimes it was an article that Cliff had read out loudly from his copy of *The Guardian* or about an issue that had recently taken place in Ashurst. But today, before anybody could say very much, in walked their boss Mr Duffy. He took Alan into his office and closed the door. What he then said was something that Alan did not want to hear.

Could Alan drop everything he was working on and fly to America to take charge of a job that one of the Dutch engineers had made a complete mess of? It was not something Alan wanted to do, because the Saints were due to play the Bradford Bulls in four days' time and the following week it was the Good Friday derby at Wigan, which he was not going to miss under any circumstances. He had to think fast how to get out of it.

"I can't break off this job I'm working on for that power station in Milan, John. It'll turn into a right mess if I have to give it to anybody else. I've also got to go down to the Mary Tavy Hydro Station possibly next week or the week after to sort out a problem there and there's an outage at Eggborough coming up next month and I've also got a hospital appointment to fit as well."

There was little that Duffy could do about all that and so he quickly left, without saying anything else about it. After he had gone, Alan came out of his office and told them all what the boss had wanted him to do and how he had talked his way out of it.

"I didn't know you were going into hospital Alan. I hope it's nothing trivial."

"It's nothing Colin, but he could have hardly challenged me on any of it, could he?"

As he started eating his lunch, he asked Jennifer if she and her sister had got any scoops for the next issue of their magazine.

"Mary has been digging around and is now convinced that there is soon going to be a massive jolt to the world banking system."

"Well, if it is only a jolt, that won't be too bad then."

"Maybe I used the wrong word."

"Maybe you did but what did she tell you?"

"I haven't really understood it all very well yet, Alan. But I'll tell you what I do know and then you can look at it on your computer at home tonight, find out a bit more and then you can tell me tomorrow."

"I'm not that clever. Go on then. Tell me what you know."

"There are two parts to it as I understand it, one specific thing and one general thing. The first is the sub-prime mortgage business in America. It began four years ago when the US banks started giving high risk loans to anybody who wanted one. At the time, their interest rates were as low as one per cent so people were easily able to pay back these loans. Now the interest rates have shot up to five per cent and many of these new home-owners are no longer able to keep up with their payments. But what the banks did some time ago was to combine these now toxic mortgages with much more secure loans which are all now no longer secure. There's more to this obviously, but according to Mary, it is leading to what might soon become a recession.

The general thing is a bit more complicated. It concerns the growth on a world scale of something called neo-liberalism."

But before she could say any more about it, Shaun stumbled into the office, carrying a large bundle of drawings. For the last week he had been working not far from Drax at Eggborough Power Station in North Yorkshire, on a job that he had just completed. He dropped the drawings onto his reference table, pulled out a hot pie he had just bought and wolfed it down.

"Have they not been feeding you proper over in Yorkshire?"

"Not with pies that are as good as Lindsay's. They must be the best pies in the whole of the North of England."

He then disappeared, returning a few minutes later with another pie and a large custard tart. As he ate it, he asked Alan what had been happening in the world while he had been away.

"Tony Blair has reshuffled his Cabinet. Charles Clarke has been dismissed as Home Secretary, Jack Straw has been replaced as Foreign Secretary by Margaret Beckett, John Prescott remains Deputy Prime Minister and Jennifer has been made editor of the *Daily Wail* and advisor to the Bank of England."

Having Shaun back in the office was good news. He could always tell a good tale about every job he had ever gone out on. His last trip abroad had been to a factory in Belgium and from where he had brought back some hilarious stories.

"How do you fancy going to America, Shaun on your next little job? If you give us a bit of that custard tart, I think that I can arrange it for you."

However Shaun didn't fancy going out on another foreign trip just yet. He had already made plans for the weekend. It was to return to Selby in East Yorkshire, where he had been lodging for the last month to fulfil a promise he had made to his landlady. It was to double check again the wiring of the light switch in her bedroom!

18

Back home and just after he had finished his tea, there was a knock on the front door. He heard Thelma answer it and then shout up to him: "Alan, it's Phil. Have you got a minute?"

Whenever Phil asked if Alan had a minute, he really meant had Alan got an hour. Inevitably it would involve some heavy physical work. Since Phil's partner Janice had moved in, just about every piece of furniture in the house had been moved, or so it seemed. Alan once said to her that it would be a good idea if anything she ever bought in future, had wheels on it. But the good thing about doing any work with Phil, was that it would always be followed by the appearance of bottles of foreign beer. And so it was tonight.

The following day passed without anything at all interesting happening at work. Cliff was out at Fiddler's Ferry again, Tariq had gone to Aberthaw Power Station and Colin had spent a good two hours in the Wiring Shop. At dinner time, Alan decided to try and understand a little more about what he had seen on his computer the previous evening.

"Jennifer, what are derivatives?"

"Why do you ask that?"

"Because I went on the internet last night to check out what you had been saying about this forthcoming financial crash in America and they are referred to quite a lot."

"I couldn't tell you off the top of my head, Alan, but our Mary has just sent me the draft of an article she has written for the next issue of *The Gap* and she makes some reference to them."

She opened up the internet on her computer and then read out what her sister had written: "A derivative is a type of contract that derives its value from the performance of an underlying entity. It can be used for a number of purposes, including insuring against price movements, increasing exposure to price movements for speculation or getting access to otherwise hard to trade markets."

She paused and then said: "Don't ask me any more about what that all that means, but does it answer your question."

"I've never heard of any of them. Do you think Mrs Thatcher knew anything about them?"

"Why do you ask that?"

"Well, she used to say that running a country's economy was just like running a little corner shop and how you can't spend more than you have got coming into the shop."

"Well, it clearly isn't. It's a hell of a lot more complicated than

19

that, believe me."

"Did she know nothing about currency speculation or British companies having their offices registered abroad in places like Jersey or Bermuda or Panama in order to avoid paying their due tax? Surely all that must also be taken into account in the operation of this country's economy."

"I agree with you Alan, and what we are going to do with *The Gap* is to bring such things to the attention of many more people. Mary has the ability to put it all into context. Not as an indifferent observer, but more like someone who can identify with all the people around the world, those who suffer wars, starvation, poverty, illness, disease and rendered powerless because of the way the financial world operates which is clearly not in the interests of most working class people like you and me and just about everybody else who lives in Ashurst."

"You know what Jennifer, you really do have a very good way with words. You are so capable of talking to lesser plebs like us lot in here. I have to tell you that I am really impressed with what you and your sister Mary do and to think that you only learned to speak proper English when you came to reside in our fair county of Lancashire."

"Thank you Alan for those kind words. They really touch my heart. Now can I leave early today? It's Bingo tonight."

4. "Why are you still voting Labour?"

The next day Alan did not manage to get much work done because he was never off the phone. First it was Cliff ringing from Fiddler's Ferry about a problem on a high voltage circuit breaker. Then Tariq rang from Aberthaw about a new control panel that had just been installed in the boiler house and wanting to know where all the equipment that it had replaced, been put. Then Horace from Wages appeared with their timesheets and as he left, Dave Morris came in with a list of the mods that he had made at a factory in Holland where he had been working for the last week. And all that was before 10 o'clock.

By the time he arrived home he was exhausted and all he felt like doing now was watching the *Six o'clock News* or *Channel Four News* or both if there was a big story breaking and if there wasn't, then listening to music. Among his favourites singers and groups were Bill Hayley and His Comets, Frankie Lane, David Whitfield, Johnny Ray, all from his teenage years, followed later by The Beatles, Thin Lizzy, Ray Charles, Bob Marley and Fleetwood Mac and more recently by Jimmy Nail, Tears for Fears, Johnny Hates Jazz, Madonna and Cher. But before he could decide what to play first, there was a loud knock on the front door.

"Please God, not Phil and that bloody sideboard again" he muttered to himself as he opened the door. However stood in front of him was not his neighbour, but a well-dressed young lady who he had never seen before. He knew why she was there though, because she was wearing a large pink rosette on her coat, clearly some bright young thing from Ashurst Labour Party.

"Good evening Mr Greenall. I am canvassing on behalf of John Marsh, the Labour Party candidate for the local election next week. I wonder if we can count on the support of yourself and Mrs Greenall?"

It seemed a long time since anybody from the Labour Party had been seen in Silkstone Street. It was probably because many of the party's old stalwarts had died or moved and had never been replaced by any younger members.

"We haven't decided yet, but I do have a couple of questions that you or he might be able to answer for me."

She nodded a little apprehensively as he said: "Why have Tony

21

Blair and Gordon Brown got this great obsession with the Private Finance Initiative system for building new schools and hospitals? Surely they must know that it is an absolute rip off for the tax-payers. Pretty lucrative for the banks though, many might say.

Secondly, why are they allowing and even encouraging private companies to get a foothold in our National Health Service? Is it their long term aim to turn it into an insurance based system like they have got in America?

Thirdly, when Alan Milburn was the Health Minister, why did he reduce the chance for the public have any say or check on what the Government was doing, by shutting down all the Community Health Councils. I know it was some time ago but when they were in existence, patients had a voice and could find out what was going on. They can't do that now, can they?"

These were not the sort of questions that she would have expected to get asked and so she had no immediate answers for any of them. So she told him that she would ask Mr Marsh and get him to call round soon to speak to him.

"Can you also find out if it's true that that bit of land where the Children's Isolation Hospital used to be, is going to get sold off on the quiet to some property developer from London?"

"I'll ask him about that as well."

"Who was that?" asked Thelma as he walked back into the living room.

"It was the Labour Party asking if me and you are going to vote for John Marsh, whoever he is."

"He's probably their candidate."

"Eh, you are probably right."

"And are you going to vote for him?"

"If I vote Labour, it means that I am voting for more of the country's wealth going into the tax havens of the super-rich, more interference in the Middle East, more reduction in the control that local government has over its housing stock, more PFIs, more privatising of the NHS and no chance of the country's industries ever being taken back into public ownership thanks to us being in the EU. Does that answer your question?"

"Well, it's given me a bit of a clue but you can tell whoever you have just been talking to that I am thinking of voting for the Green Party candidate, if there is one standing."

"He was not standing at the front door when I just shut it but

22

they do have a candidate standing this time. Do you know what his name is?"

"No."

"It's Ken Brown."

"Do you know anything about him?"

"Yes, I do. His dad Arthur, was in my night school class when we were both doing our Higher National at St Helens Tech. They lived up Shaley Brow then and when I knew them, they were a very colourful family."

"Really. Why was that?"

"His mother's maiden name was White. For a long time Ken was going out with a girl called Amber from Blackbrook. He had a brother who married a girl from Red House Lane in Astley and a cousin who lived at Goose Green in Wigan."

"You are making all that up."

"I bet you didn't know that when I was a lad, when they had elections in Ashurst, they never used to count the votes."

"Really, why not?"

"They used to weigh them."

"The old ones are always the best."

"Do you mean like me?"

"Aye lad, aye."

"I often wondered what happened to Arthur. He used to be an electrician with MANWEB, but he'll be retired by now."

"Talking of people being retired, when are you going to start doing a bit more on your family tree?"

"Why do you ask?"

"Because a new girl has just started working with us in the shop and her surname is Pickavance. You have said to me before that there is someone called Pickavance in your family tree. Perhaps you might be related to her."

"Is she under 40, good looking, nice legs and English."

"No. She's Welsh just like little me and she has only just come to live in Ashurst."

"Where does she come from?"

"Llanfairpwllgwyngllgogerychwynrndrobwyll."

"Where?"

"Near Bangor."

"I have been thinking of doing a bit more on it. I think I might start after I have had my tea or do you want me to wash up?"

23

"It's done. By the way, Robert was talking to me on the phone, this afternoon about something that Megan has just discovered. What do you know about a man called Norman Bethune?"

"He was a Canadian doctor who fought in the Spanish Civil War on the Republican side. Later he went to China, worked with the Chinese Red Army and actually knew Mao Tse Tung. Why?"

"Because Megan thinks she might be related to him."

"Why does she think that?"

"A few weeks ago, her aunt, who had spent much of her early life living abroad, died. Last week Megan went over to Wrexham to help her cousin Melanie clear her house out. Among the stuff they found were a lot of foreign stamps, some very old Chinese coins, pamphlets about the Spanish Civil War and some very old books including one in which was written on the first page, a name that was something like Mick Bathund or Mick Bethune.

"Megan has details of her family tree going back a long way and it includes a woman who went to live in Canada over 100 years ago and married a man called Arthur whose surname was something like that in Toronto in 1910. Megan also discovered it was not far from where Norman Bethune had grown up and around the same time too. So there is a slight chance that there may be a family connection with your Norman Bethune."

"Very interesting, so when are they coming over again?"

"They are coming on Sunday for a meal so you can ask her then. And after that, you can try and find out if there are any more revolutionary historical heroes with close links to the great Greenall proletarian dynasty."

Alan had always had a big interest in history. It included the history of the planet, the history of Ashurst and the history of his own family.

His interest in the planet had come from what he had learned from their former tea girl, Hazel Hutton. In 1972 she had gone to Bradford College in Yorkshire with the aim of becoming a teacher. While she had been there, she had developed an interest in geology and the writings of one James Hutton. He was a 17th century Scottish landowner who had tried being a lawyer, a doctor and a farmer before finding his true vocation as a scientist.

According to Hazel, he could even be classed as important as Copernicus, Galileo and Newton in helping free science from the dogma of religion and in his case determining scientifically the

24

history and origins of the Earth. His research had enabled him to prove that it was clearly over four billion years old.

His interest in the history of Ashurst and its surrounding towns came firstly from his own experiences, visiting other local factories where the company's electrical and electronic products had been installed. It also came from tales told by some of his relatives and many of his old mates about where they had once worked.

As a result in addition to about 20 factories in Ashurst, most of which had now been demolished, Alan also knew a lot about ICI at Widnes, Vulcan Foundry at Newton le Willows, TT Vicars at Earlestown and Pilkington's Glass Works in St Helens. He also had two mates who worked for the National Coal Board, one in the Wages Department at Bold Colliery, the other an electrician who was very pally with another electrician, the former Saints second-row Cumbrian forward Dick Huddart.

He had first started work on the family tree during the 1962 to 1963 winter, at a time when he had been off work after having been injured playing football for Astley United. At the time, many older relatives were still alive and were able to provide him with information about other family members who they knew about. In those days nobody had a computer and most things that he discovered came by word of mouth. Now he was in a much better position to check everything on the internet.

Until Alan's grandfather was 11, the Holding family had lived at Fingerpost in St Helens. Then they had moved a few miles to Ashurst when Alan's great grandfather had got a job as a drawer at Bank Top. That was also the time when his grandfather had finished school and begun his working life at the nearby Southport Edge pit.

After spending most of the First World War in a prisoner of war camp east of Berlin, Ned had returned home and after two more years working underground, he had left and gone to work at Mather's Foundry, finishing his time there as a shop foreman.

Two relatives on his mother's side of the family were his uncle Jack who had worked as a fitter, first at Davis Pumps, then at Dawson's Chocolate Works and Jarratt Machine Tool, all in Ashurst and finally at UGB in St Helens and also his uncle Billy who had only ever worked as a sheeter at Hilton's Assembly.

Going much further back, Alan had discover details of Arthur Silas Holding a collier who had been born at Collins Green in 1791.

On his grandmother's side of the family, Alan had managed to get as far back as 1803 when the watch maker William Tabern had been born in Prescot, one of five children.

Alan also knew that his great grandmother had been born at Pocket Nook in St Helens in 1860 and had died when his grandmother was around 10 years old. It was at that point in her young life that she had to finish going to school and become the little mother for the rest of the Tabern family.

Sadly, he knew little about his own father who had been killed in the war at Monte Cassino in Italy. It was his uncle Jack though who had been almost like a father to him. Alan knew that one of the best things he had ever done for him, was to take him to watch the Saints when he was just seven years old. He had done much more for him too and so had auntie Doris. Maybe their actions had compensated for the fact that their first child, their son Gerald had died from TB in 1941.

The phone rang. It was Rebecca wanting to speak to her mother and so Alan knew that even if it was only a short conversation, it would still last a long time. So he went upstairs and googled in the words globalisation and neo-liberalism to see how much they were dominating the world economy.

Two hours later he came downstairs to watch the *Ten o'clock News*. While he had been upstairs, Thelma had also been on the phone to Dorothy, the wife of his brother Paul. They now lived in Spain and it looked as though Paul might soon have to go into hospital. When *The News* was over, he turned to Thelma and said: "When you first set foot in Ashurst, did you ever think that you would still be here 50 years later, at the centre of a family with a husband, two children, two grandchildren, over at least a dozen other relatives and 17 Saints to support?"

"Well, actually it's going to be a bit more than that."

"What do you mean?"

"I've just been on the phone to Megan. She rang me while you were upstairs. She's told me that she's expecting."

"You mean she's expecting to turn up on Saturday on time, for a change."

But he knew exactly what she meant.

26

5. Them bloody stupid pliers

Just as Alan was about to leave the house the next day, the phone rang. It was Cliff wanting him to come straight over to Fiddler's Ferry because he needed some help in the Control Room. It was a job that would only take an hour if it was done today, but it would take the rest of the week if it was not done today. Alan was due to have a meeting with their boss Mr Duffy that morning but that would have to wait. And if it couldn't wait, then tough.

When he got back into work that afternoon, Jennifer told him that Duffy had cancelled their meeting anyway and gone to Swindon for yet another meeting with National Power. She was now tidying all the papers on her desk, something she usually saved for the last day before the start of the Works Fortnight or the Christmas holidays. It was because just before he had left, Duffy had told her to hold fire on whatever she was working on and wait for his further instructions. In other words do nothing until she heard otherwise.

A good time to ask her a few more questions about what he had seen on his computer the previous evening, Alan thought. But before he could speak to her, he was called down to the Assembly Shop and by the time he returned, she had gone home.

Soon after they had finished their evening meal, Robert and Megan arrived. Congratulations were the order of the day and a little bit of maternity talk from Thelma too. No doubt there would be a lot more of that, over the next nine months or more likely the next nine years or probably even more.

Then Thelma brought them all back to earth when she asked: "Are you two going to get married, now?"

"How much will it cost and will I have to buy a tie?"

"It depends what you have Robert, where you have it and a few other things as well."

But before any more could be said, the phone rang. It was Rebecca wanting to know if the children could stay over the following night. By the time that conversation had finished, Megan and Robert had left.

Alan then switched on his computer and started looking into some of the things that Jennifer had recently told him about how the world economy operated. The subject was beginning to interest him as he read about how money, maybe better described as finance capital, was moved around the world by its owners in order to maximise their profits, irrespective of how it might affect the lives of lots of other people. His interest was also a very personal thing for him too. His capital, if you can call £251 capital, was in the Ashurst branch of Northern Rock. Surely that would always be safe. Or would it?

Soon it was time to watch the *Ten o'clock News*. The main item covered the charging of Saddam Hussein with war crimes, and was followed by an interview with Tony Blair with him again justifying why he knew that he was right to lead the country into the invasion of Iraq in 2003. He also spoke of the need for major investment in the North of England but now, whatever he said about anything, few people would ever believe him again.

The next day, Jennifer asked Alan what he had learned from his recent research. Then she talked a bit more about commodity trading, futures, derivatives, long selling, short selling, currency exchanges and swaps. He was still quite baffled by it all, but there was one thing that she had mentioned a couple of times before and which he was familiar with and from a very early age too.

"I know all about swaps."

"Really, Alan. I am impressed."

"It's from the time when I was living at home in Chisnall Avenue. I used to swap comics every week with three of my mates. That's how I got to read *Adventure*, *Rover*, *Wizard* and *Radio Fun* every week.

"And do you still read them?"

He laughed and went on: "I knew a lot about profits too because at Sunday School every week, they kept telling us stories about the prophets. Then Jesus must have fallen out with the money lenders because one day he knocked their tables over. After that, he said that unless you follow me, there will be no futures for any of you."

At this point Mr Duffy walked in. Alan could tell by his general demeanour that he wanted something doing and Alan expected it would involve him having to travel to some faraway place in the world. He was partly right, because it was actually to two faraway places in the world.

It was a request for him to visit two cotton mills where the company had recently installed some textile machinery. The first was a few miles east of Portugal's second largest city of Porto and the other was in Morocco. He knew the one at Familicao well. He

28

had visited it twice and had always enjoyed his time there, mainly because of the people he had to deal with.

There was Emilio the electrician, Gaspar the shop foreman, Raul the odd job man who was always called on when anything heavy needed moving or lifting and Giuseppe the Italian, who ran the Drawing Office. The only thing that he knew about the second mill came from an electrician who had been there twice and had told Alan that the place was on the edge of the desert, the food was good and the mill manager was a Wiganer from Ince.

But when he arrived there a few days later, he discovered there had been some big changes. Emilio had gone to work at the company's other mill a few kilometres away, Gaspar had retired, Raul was working in a circus in Madrid and Giuseppe was now living with a rich widow and her little dog called Gizmo in Porto. The electrician he had to deal with was Estevo. He spoke quite good English and was dead easy to get on with, but the boss now was Filipe who nobody seemed to like.

Alan spent a week there and probably put on half a stone, being unable to resist what was served free in the canteen every lunch time and drinking far too much brandy with the area being at the heart of whatever is used to distil that drink. Then, standing in Reception and literally minutes before he was due to leave the hotel and go by taxi to the airport to fly to Casablanca, there was a telephone call for him.

"Alan, it's Cliff. There's been a terrible disaster here."

Alan froze. Whatever could it be? He could only think the worst, something involving one of his family.

"What is it?"

"We all think you've left a cheese butty in the drawer in your office. It's smelling summat rotten and we can't find the key. Do you know where it is?"

"Phew. Thank goodness for that. So what's the story?"

"There's been a big fire at that mill in Morocco so don't go there. Stay in Portugal for a couple more days as Duffy might want you to go to that bottle works in Spain, before you come back."

As a result of this call, he spent the next three days walking round Porto and then on the fourth day after a long phone call with Duffy, he took a taxi almost to the centre of the city, not quite though but to Aeroporto Porto and five hours later, he was back home in Ashurst with a load of stories to tell.

29

One thing he always enjoyed on returning home was listening to Thelma tell him what had happened while he had been away to other members of their family and also to any of their neighbours.

Some new people had moved in a week earlier. Their new home had been occupied since 1946 by the Faircloughs. For the last few years though, only Mrs Fairclough had lived there, with all the other relatives either having moved away or died. Now she had gone to join them, after spending the last few weeks of her life in Whiston Hospital.

"Have you met the new neighbours yet?"

"Yes. I have."

"I thought you would have. What are they like?"

"It's quite a nice couple in their 50s and they both have a car. They also have a daughter who lives at Winwick who has already been half a dozen times in her car and another relative who came and stayed the weekend. The good news is that he doesn't have a car. The bad news is that he's got a very noisy motorbike."

"Charming."

"Indeed."

"What's his wife like?"

"She's not his wife. She just lives with him."

"You mean they are living over the brush."

"What?"

"Living over the brush. Have you never heard that before? It means two people who are not married, living together in the same house. It's shocking. It will bring utter shame on our whole street."

"Tell that to Robert and Megan."

"Where were they living before?"

"You'll like this. In Mulberry Avenue near St Luke's Church in St Helens. And do you know what. He was in the year below Cliff at Knowsley Road School."

"What's his surname?"

"Kenilworth."

"I'll tell Cliff about that tomorrow. Anyway, that's enough about that. Let's open this bottle of wine and I'll tell you about Portugal. It's from Estevo's own vineyard."

He talked about his time at the mill, obviously ignoring all the technical problems he had dealt with and then about Estevo. It was clear the two of them had got on very well together.

"He had an English mother and a Portuguese father and they

lived in Lisbon until he was 12. That was when his father died and his mother brought Estevo back to England. When he was 16 he started as an apprentice with a GEC firm in Wembley called Witton James that manufactured printing press drives and auto paster reel stands. When it got closed down, he went back to Portugal and later married a lady from Porto.

"At the weekend he invited me round to his place and on the Saturday evening there was a football match on the TV. So we watched it but it bored me stiff."

"'Don't you like football?' he asked."

"'No' I said. I'd rather watch rugby and then he amazed me with his response:"

"'Which do you prefer, league or union?'"

"So I told him that I was a big rugby league fan. Then he surprised me by telling me that when he worked at Witton James, he was very pally with a draughtsman called Geoff who came from St Helens and so he always went with him to watch the Challenge Cup Final. He also had a girlfriend who was a student at the LSE at the time and came from Eccles and so each time they went up north to see her family, they always went to watch Swinton play."

Back at work Alan wasted over an hour of the following morning explaining what he had done at Familicao to Mr Duffy. Then he went down to the Wiring Shop to sort out some modifications to a control panel. It should have taken him no more than 10 minutes with the shop foreman, but Albert kept getting called away to his phone to sort out problems in the Turbine Hall at West Burton Power Station.

While Alan was standing there waiting for Albert to reappear, he listened to Jimmy, one of the wiremen talking about a couple of former Wilkinson's employees who had recently been in the local paper for some anti-social behaviour. It was Tony Hanson and his wife Alma, both of whom Alan knew in the 1960s and 70s. But then just about everybody who had ever worked at Wilkinson's knew about the Hansons as did nearly everybody who lived in Nook End.

At that time, every summer the firm held The Managers' Ball at a large hotel in Southport. It was a very select affair, a meal followed by a dance and a room for the night. It was the custom for all those foremen who might be considered suitable for promotion, to be invited to this social event along with their wives.

However, someone must have made a mistake because not only were Tony and Alma invited when he was only a chargehand, but for some strange reason, they had both been put on the top table, along with Basil Wilkinson and his wife, Basil's brother Norman and his wife, the company secretary along with the main guest for the evening. That particular year, it had been a famous Lord from Westminster accompanied by his lady friend, somebody who had probably never travelled much further north than Watford in her whole life before.

By the time they had all moved from the bar to the main hall and sat down for the meal, Tony had drunk three pints of mixed and was now clearly in top form. As the food was put before them, he saw a large bowl of pickled walnuts on the table. Then he watched as everybody began picking them up, carefully using a pair of silver tongs.

Unfortunately he was no longer sober enough by now to use these tongs very well. On his third attempt he finally succeeded in lifting one small walnut up, but he soon lost control of it. It shot across the table and landed on the cleavage of the gracious lady from mid-Surrey. Everybody went quiet except for Alma. Well known as a loudmouth and a lot more too, she shouted out for everybody else to hear: "Why don't you use your fingers like you do when you are at home instead of them bloody stupid pliers?"

Jimmy also lived in Nook End and frequently drank in The Bull, which was also the Hansons' local. He then began to tell Alan of an incident involving Alma playing bowls under the floodlights one night with an Australian rugby league player. But before he could get to the punch line, which was about what happened after all the floodlights had been turned off, Albert the foreman came out of his office, apologised for all his interruptions, and spent the next quarter of an hour sorting everything out to both his and Alan's satisfaction.

6. Dining out in London with a Lord

It was 26 August and Thelma's birthday. She was now 62 years old, although she looked more like a woman approaching her mid-50s. Usually she and Alan would have celebrated the day at home with Rebecca and Robert, their partners and their children, but not today. The two of them were in London sitting with their neighbours Phil and Janice and accompanied by a lot of other people, a few of whom they knew well, a few they knew a little and a lot who they did not know at all. It was a very nice day for such a celebration, but at an unusual location. It was indeed a very odd location for any member of the Greenall family because it was the North Stand of Twickenham, the home of English rugby union, although today it was not to watch any rugby union.

They were sitting there in a crowd of over 65,000 people for the Rugby League Challenge Cup Final between St Helens and the Huddersfield Giants. Most of the people around them were clearly Saints fans, though not all of them. Directly in front were an oldish couple from Dewsbury and further along that row was a group of noisy young men from Barrow-in-Furness.

Then a voice called out her name. She looked around to see who it was and saw Big Joan, who had once been in charge of the Print Room at work. She was a friend who Thelma had not seen for ages. She looked really old now, but still had that cheeky grin on her face. She took a piece of paper out of her handbag, wrote on it and passed it to the man sat behind her, indicating that it had to be passed on. It was a telephone number starting with the numbers 01942. Clearly Joan must have moved from her old house in Shaley Brow and gone to live in Wigan. But clearly she was still a Saint, always had been, always would be.

Thelma was now standing up looking around her to see if she could see anybody else who she knew. She did, but they were all too far away to call to. Slowly, the row behind them began to fill up and, as she sat down, she became aware of two women sat behind her, chattering away. At first she could not make out what they were saying, but as time went on, she realised that they were both speaking in Welsh. She turned round, smiled at them and asked where they were from.

"I'm from Treorchy and Janet here is from Maesteg. Why? You

33

sound a little bit Welsh yourself. Where are you from?"

"Tonyrefail."

"Are you? My brother lives in Tonyrefail. Maybe you know him. He's a bus driver, Johnny Davis. Where do you live? I haven't seen you around before."

Thelma had to explain that she had only lived in Tonyrefail until her mother had died in 1945 when she was less than one year old and had then been brought up in a home in Cardiff and now lived in Ashurst which was quite near to St Helens. She suddenly felt a strong link with them both. They were Welsh like she was, probably a similar age, obviously rugby league fans like she was and their accents were very pleasing to listen to. Then Thelma asked them who they were supporting today.

"Oh, the Saints of course. One of our family played for them some time ago. Scott Gibbs. He'll probably be here somewhere, I guess. Although I haven't seen him for ages."

Then the other woman chipped in: "My brother used to play union with Kel Coslett, when he was at Aberavon. He was your full-back once, though he must be getting on a bit now."

Then the first woman, almost proudly, spoke again: "We are all rugby league fans in our family. My dad prefers it now to union and he once played for Wales, a long time ago."

Then Alan chipped in with a few words of very badly spoken Welsh. The woman, rubbed her hand over his head and said: "I don't think this one is one of ours."

Turning back to Thelma, she went on: "I always like coming to your Cup Final. Always such a good atmosphere and there's never any trouble either. I really enjoy it."

Then, a man now standing next to her said to her loudly: "There'll be some trouble if you don't let me get past. I'm dying for a pee."

The players were now entering the field and soon it became clear that the Challenge Cup would be heading back to Lancashire with the Saints winning easily 42–12 with Sean Long winning the Lance Todd Trophy, as man-of-the-match, for the third time in his career.

Until the Challenge Cup had been presented, they remained seated, letting everybody else leave with most of them having to start the long journey back up north. That's what they would also have done normally, but not today because they were staying in

London for the night. This was because of a telephone conversation that Alan had had earlier in the month, with Scott who had once spent part of his five year trade apprenticeship in Wilkinson's Drawing Office.

Scott was now living in London, with a young lady called Celia who worked for ITV. Knowing that Alan would be in London for the Cup Final, he had rung to invite him and whoever he was with, to come to Celia's birthday party and stay the night.

So little more than half an hour after leaving Twickenham, Phil was driving onto the forecourt of what looked more like a mansion than a large house. As he switched the engine off, Scott came out of the front door. After saying how pleased he was to see the four of them, he went on to tell them to prepare themselves for a bit of a shock. They were coming to a birthday party, the like of which none of them would have ever have been to before.

"Her parents are both here, her father is a Lord and her mother has a top job in the Foreign Office. Her brother and his wife will be here as well. He works at the Board of Trade and she's a journalist for a couple of society magazines. Her cousin Martine might turn up with her friend Elizabeth as well if they can get back from filming in Cornwall, she's quite a famous actress, you see."

"The thing is they are all very nice in their own way, but somehow they are not the sort of people you would ever find living in a town like Ashurst. So you just behave and talk like you normally do and it will be a bit of an eye opener for them all."

Then he said to Alan: "I bet you have never been with a Lord before."

"Wrong again Scott, like you always were when you were drawing those little brackets for me. I once met Lord Lofthouse when I was on a job at Eggborough. One of the lads on our gang I was out with one night, introduced me to him, in a pub in Sharlston. He even bought us both a pint."

And then he went on to describe a member of the aristocracy in very glowing terms, when he said: "He's a big Featherstone Rovers fan, you know."

They walked into the house and straight into the main room. Dominating it was a large table with chairs for at least a dozen people. Celia introduced them all to her mother and father, then her brother Miles and his wife Pamela, her cousin Martine and the actress Elizabeth who was clearly a little bit more than a friend.

35

Celia indicated where everybody should sit and then proceeded to ring a small bell which was the signal for two maids to bring in the food. Then some very polite conversation commenced with Mother asking her daughter if she had found a good gardener yet. Father said that their housekeeper had gone back to live in Italy and they were struggling at the moment without her.

This was followed by Pamela, saying that she had a problem finding someone suitable to look after her little dog. She was away from the house such a lot at the moment on Royal duties and the poor thing was just not getting the attention that it deserved. The early conversations were quite dull with their guests from the north thoroughly enjoying the food and particularly the wine.

Then Father asked Alan a question. By this time he was now feeling like introducing an element of shop floor humour into the evening's proceedings.

"Alan, I believe that you were once in charge of the Drawing Office where young Scott worked for a while. What was he like? Was he much of a draughtsman?"

"Scott was definitely a one-off. He is the only draughtsman I know that can have a 19 core cable with 19 wires going in at one end and 20 wires coming out at the other end."

Father wasn't quite sure of the statement so he just smiled as Alan continued: "He once worked on a big cabling job for me and although he was still only an apprentice then, he got it 99 per cent correct."

"Very good" said Father "So he wasn't just a pretty face."

"You can say that though not many others would. You see, I left him to organise the running of a heavy armoured power cable from the substation to the main fuseboard in the Copper Refinery over a weekend. I estimated it would have to be about 200 metres long, but I left him to do all the measuring up.

"Well, he did all the measuring, ordered the cable, got it cut to length and wound onto a cable drum. Then a gang of men started to drop it into the cable trenches that had been dug for it. It was spot on at the substation end. It dropped in perfectly but at the other end it was just two yards short."

Father then indicated that he did not quite appreciate the significance of this when he said: "Quite near then."

"That's not what the foreman said, did he Scott?"

Thelma laughed out loud although she had heard this story

before. Phil and Janice did as well but no-one else did. Maybe they had never seen all the hard work being carried out by a gang of men pulling a four core 25 square millimetre, steel wire armoured copper power cable in pouring rain before and then right at the end discovering all their efforts had all been in vain.

Maybe they thought Alan was having a go at young Scott. But then they probably would not have appreciated that having a right go at one of your mates was a very Lancashire thing. It used to go on all the time at work.

Like the time the draughtsman Frank Taylor from Clinkham Wood had struggled into work one day with a broken ankle and had to spend every day for the next six weeks sat in front of his reference table and never being able to go out on site.

"Look on the bright side, Frank" Charlie, the office comedian from Thatto Heath, had said to him loudly.

"When you are at home now, you'll have a good excuse to tell your Maud why you can't do any washing up."

At this point the phone went. It was someone wishing Celia happy birthday. By the time she had returned to the table, her brother had brought the conversation down to a very mundane level when he asked if anybody knew why there had been so much traffic around Twickenham. He was sure that England did not have a match today.

"It was the Rugby League Challenge Cup" said Father "that's where our honoured guests have been to this afternoon."

"Really. I didn't know they were allowed to play that game at Twickers."

"Well it would not have happened in my day. But then things have changed although not necessarily for the better, I would say."

Celia's sister-in-law Pamela, then said that her husband Miles used to play rugby. Now ready to join in, Thelma asked whether it was league or union that he had played.

It was clear Pamela did not know as she looked at her husband and asked rather stupidly whether he knew.

"Union of course. We don't play rugby league down here. It's only played in a few small towns up North."

This is my chance, thought Alan. This could be interesting.

"Miles, I don't think that you are quite right there. Have you never heard of London Broncos or London Skolars or West London Sharks or South London Storm? There's a lot of rugby league being

37

played in all the schools here as well. In fact I have heard that there are as many school kids playing the game in London as play it in Bradford."

"Really, I didn't think the education authorities would allow it."

"Why not?"

Then Martine chipped in: "It's only a professional game, isn't it. How could children play? How would they get paid?"

"Do children in the London schools play Soccer because that's a professional game as well?

"Well how can the adults play it for money? Nobody ever watches it down here. Where would all the money come from?"

"Plenty of adults play Soccer on Hackney Marshes on a Sunday morning. They don't get paid, do they?"

Then Father spoke again: "When I played at Wasps you were not even allowed to enter the club house if you had once played rugby league."

Always keen to give one of his little history talks about his favourite sport Alan then told an interesting story that none of Celia's entourage had ever heard before.

"I'll tell you what things were once like. In the 1930s, Bristol had a full-back named Brown who was often in the England rugby union team. At some point in his life he decided that he might like to try rugby league and so he came up to Warrington and met some of their club's officials. After a long conversation he decided not to proceed with the idea and went back home.

"Sometime later, the rugby union authorities found out what he had done and banned him from playing for life, just for talking about swapping codes. That was in the mid-1930s and do you know when he saw his first ever live game of rugby league? It was nearly 20 years later, sat in his front room in Bristol watching it on *Grandstand* one Saturday afternoon."

Then Father showed some genuine interest in the discussion when he said: "We all know how rugby started. It was when that clever young student at Rugby School picked the ball up and ran with it. But how did rugby league start? Was it because the players all wanted paying?"

It was Alan's cue again: "If you are referring to William Webb Ellis, that was not true. It was just a myth created by the Establishment to try and keep it as a sport for gentlemen around the time of the split in 1895.

38

He went on to explain how association football and then rugby had established agreed sets of rules for their sport and how the Football Association had managed to accommodate amateurs and professionals in one organisation. But in rugby, the sport's leadership saw how the teams from the industrial areas had come to dominate their sport, and were determined to avoid such a thing happening. Playing for cups and in league competitions, combined with the issue of 'broken time' – compensating players who lost money when they had to miss a Saturday morning shift at work, led to the formation of the Northern Union in 1895, which later became Rugby League.

"Well, I never knew all that" said Father. "I have really learned a lot today. The next time I see that fellow from Wakefield, I'll have to apologise to him for what I have said to him over the years. Do any of you know him?"

"If you mean David Hinchcliffe, I don't know him personally but I do know he's written a book about it."

"What is it called?"

"*Rugby's Class War*. And if you are really interested in what happened at the George there is an account of it in a book called *Rugby's Great Split*, written by a historian called Tony Collins."

"Will they be in the library?"

And with that, he smiled at Alan and then said: "Does anybody mind if I smoke?"

And before anybody could say they did, he brought out a large cigar and lit up and then asked the rest of the family if he had told them of his holiday plans for the summer.

But before Father could start to dominate the proceedings again, Alan decided that he would get the last word in on the subject and said: "If you want to know a little bit about how and why rugby league came to be the most popular sport in Australia, have a look at a book called *The Rugby Rebellion*. It's written by an Australian called Sean Fagan. It really is a very interesting read."

7. "I follow Marlborough League"

The party finished just before midnight. It had been dominated by Father. After the maids had cleared the table, he started talking about his forthcoming holiday. This would begin in a large cottage that he owned in the French Alps, continue in a hotel in Monte Carlo for a fortnight and finish with a week in Barcelona. He certainly loved the sound of his own voice and was so full of himself that it was amazing that Alan had not countered with some clever play on words to bring him down a peg.

He then went on to bore them with a few tales about his wartime experiences in Italy and for no apparent reason made some pretty disparaging comments about all the Greeks that he had ever had the misfortune to meet during those troubled times. And it was from Thelma that he probably received what was the greatest put down he had had for a very long time, when she quietly said: "My father was Greek."

Father tried to diffuse the situation by saying that he didn't mean that all the people from Greece were bad, just those that he had known personally. Then, he suggested that they should all now play his favourite game which was "Are you man who?"

What the four guests from the North had now come to appreciate was, that whatever Father suggested should be done, was more of a command than a suggestion and that any games he suggested that they should play, they had to let him win.

They had planned to leave around nine o'clock the following morning, but none of them were even awake at that unearthly hour. They had a late breakfast-early lunch and around midday finally left, with Janice driving and Thelma sat with her in the front. As they saw the first sign post for the M6, Phil said: "I was impressed by the way you told his Lordship about the origins of Rugby League, Alan. Have you been studying it at night school?"

"When I was an apprentice, an electrician I worked with quite a lot on nights, played for Liverpool Stanley just after the war. One of our neighbours in Chisnall Avenue played for St Helens Recs during their last season in 1938 and the uncle of one of my schoolmates had been a referee in Widnes in the 1930s. Listening to all these people talk about the game kicked off my interest in its history. Then I started buying the *Rugby Leaguer* every week and this led on to me buying books about the game. Mind you, there were very few books published then, unlike now with loads being published every year."

"So if I wanted to know about the history of rugby league, what would you suggest I start with?"

Thelma turned round sharply and said: "*Tries in the Valleys*". That's the first one I ever read."

"It depends where you want to start, Phil. What Thelma has just mentioned is a good read, but it is set sometime after 1895 and it just covers the game in South Wales. You might be better starting with what led up to that first meeting in the George Hotel in Huddersfield in 1895. There is quite a lot written about it."

"So you lend me a book about that tomorrow and I'll try and read it within three months and then I'll give it back to you."

"Three months. How slow a reader are you?"

"Eh Alan, I only went to a secondary modern, not like you posh grammar school boys."

"I think that the best one to start on would be *Rugby's Great Split* which is what I told his Nibs about last night. It covers the background to the causes of the split which was partly over the issue of broken time payment and also the issue of class."

"Well that doesn't surprise me."

"What?"

"The fact that the issue of class is involved. Why is it with you that most things in this life are affected by or related to class?"

"Maybe because it's true."

"Tell me a couple of other books and then I can chose."

"Tony Collins, who wrote *Rugby's Great Split,* has also written another one called *Rugby League in Twentieth Century Britain*."

"That might be better. Unlike you, I didn't live before the First World War."

"Tell him about *Rugby League in its own Words*."

It was Thelma again suggesting another book that she had enjoyed reading too.

"It's a very unusual book is that one, Phil. It's written by a lad from Leeds called Phil Wilkinson and one from Billinge called Ray Gent. It portrays rugby league as though it was a real live person and a member of a big family."

"I didn't know there were any clever folk like that up Billinge"

"You want to get out a bit more, Phil."

41

"Maybe I should. Do Hattons run coach trips there?"

"No, but Arriva do. Every half hour on the way to Wigan."

"So if I read those two books, will I become as clever as you are?"

"You might do."

"So what else is there?"

"*The Forbidden Game* by Mike Rylance describes how rugby league grew in France in the 1930s and was then banned by the French Vichy government during the German occupation."

"Looks like I am going to have to give up painting."

"And washing up and hoovering" chipped in Janice.

"A very interesting book for you might be the biography of the Saints centre, the legendary Duggie Greenall."

"I'll start on that. I've met him a few times when he came to our house. My dad used to be pals with him when they both worked at Triplex."

It was clear that Phil was going to enjoy reading about the game that he had watched for nearly 50 years and so he went on: "Did Ashurst ever have a rugby team, Alan?"

"From what I have read, Ashurst was more of a football town. It was a bit like Earlestown. There were two rugby teams in the town in the 1880s. If they had joined together they might have been invited to send a delegate to that meeting at the George."

Then he continued with one of his favourite stories about rugby league history: "Did you like it when I told his Nibs that the origins of the game had nothing to do with what is said to have happened at Rugby School around 1820?"

"I did."

"I was going to ask him what did he think might have happened if William Webb Ellis had not gone to Rugby Public School but had gone to Marlborough Public School instead."

"What would have happened if he had?"

"I would now have to tell people that I am a big Marlborough League fan."

Then Alan laughed and went on: "I sometimes wonder what might have happened if William Webb Ellis had gone to the same public school that I went to."

"You never went to a public school."

"I did, Lane Head Junior school."

But before Phil could reply, Janice slowed down, drove onto the

42

hard shoulder and stopped.

"What's up? Have we run out of gas?" he asked.

Janice said nothing to him but started reversing and slowly approached three Saints fan stood alongside a fairly old car.

"It's your brother Jack, Phil."

It was indeed Phil's brother Jack stood there with his wife Angie and another man. Angie was a nurse at Wrightington Hospital and was due to start work at six o'clock. So it was decided that she came back with them while Jack and Ken waited for the AA to arrive and deal with the car's problem. And so as a result of Janice keeping her eyes firmly on the road and the hard shoulder too, Angie managed to get to work on time and later helped save the life of an old lady from Crank.

First thing the next day, Alan was asked by Duffy if he could go to a firm in Accrington that had just placed an order for an electronic weighing machine and a conveyor belt system. Alan said that he could and so Duffy made two phone calls and within 20 minutes, Alan was on his way.

The engineer he met there was a man called Cedric. He was a very friendly guy, with a broad East Lancashire accent, and on the wall of his office were three photographs indicating that he was also a crown green bowler.

Alan looked at the way Cedric had sketched out the new arrangement and immediately saw there was a much better way of doing the whole job.

"Can I ask you a few simple questions about this job?"

"Aye, lad."

"How many women work here?"

"There's six altogether and they all work in the General Office which is right at the front of the building. Why do you ask that? Do you want one right now?"

Alan laughed and then asked how many people came to work on a bike. It was none.

"Right. Do you want to hear of a better layout and place to put this weighing machine?"

Cedric nodded and said that he did.

"Knock down the ladies toilets, the bike sheds and that doorway. Reposition the main fuseboard there. Then you can put the weighing machine where the main fuseboard is now. This will make it easier for us to do our work and you will probably no longer need

43

to cart stuff upstairs to be weighed and processed and then brought down again."

"That all sounds pretty good to me. I wonder why I hadn't thought of it myself" said Cedric.

"Let's say that in our first discussion, you did come up with the idea. And then I can say that I just went along with it and suggested an easier and cheaper way to do it."

"I'll tell the boss what we have discussed and you can give us a price for it, but as far as I am concerned, the job is yours."

Driving back home after having enjoyed the time he had spent with Cedric, Alan thought about what he had done. The way the place would operate after the new scheme was up and running, would probably mean three things. The production process in the plant would be more efficient. This would lead to a higher turnover and an increase in profits for the owners. Automating the plant in this way, might also lead to the need for less workers. In other words automation would lead to more unemployment, even if it was only one or two men who were no longer needed. Looked at in that way, Alan knew that he was to blame.

"It's the old problem with capitalism as ever," he thought to himself. "Production for profit, not production for social need".

He thought about many jobs he had worked on over the years. Installing new high tech machinery and control systems always had the inevitable result of machinery doing the work that humans once did. In other words more men and women would be put out of work. As he mulled over the issue the miles flew past and it was not long before he saw the sign post for Ashton in Makerfield.

He saw that a lot of cars in front of him were coming off the motorway there. Clearly there was some hold up further down the motorway he thought so he decided to turn off there and within half an hour he was sat in his favourite chair.

That evening, details of an accident on the M6 were covered on Radio Merseyside. It involved a man who had been knocked off his motorbike while overtaking a lorry. And where did the unfortunate young man come from? It was Accrington. Another little Charlie Eccleston coincidence, Alan thought to himself.

After they had finished their tea, they decided to go bowling in Victoria Park. As they walked along Newton Street they saw a couple in the distance crossing the road. It was Pete Mulholland with his wife Ann. Straight away they changed their plans and

44

decided to all go for a drink. Alan suggested going to *The Ring o'
Bells*, but Pete thought that was not a very good idea.

"It'll be snooing with young uns in there tonight. They've got
Ricky Nelson on. We'll be better going to the Prescot."

The Prescot Arms was the only pub that Alan had ever been
clotched from, clotched being the Ashurst word for barred. He didn't
think that would stop him having a drink in there tonight though,
as Big Dave the landlord then, no longer worked there. In fact he
had not been worked there for over 30 years because he had died
in a boating accident on holiday in Cornwall in 1975.

Soon they were joined by Pete's neighbours Betty and her
husband Tim, along with a man they did not know. It was Betty's
cousin who had just returned from America and was now looking
for a place to either rent or buy in Ashurst. He had recently seen
one that he quite liked in Silkstone Street, but his comments about
it, indicated what his general attitude to life was. It was after Betty
had told him that Alan and Thelma had both enjoyed living there
since 1988.

"So I take it that it's not full of nig nogs then" was John's first
comment and then he went on to say that the main reason that he
had returned from America was because there were far too many
blacks and Mexicans living there for his liking.

"Well if you don't like foreigners John, you won't like living in our
street. It's got loads of Welsh and Irish people there already."

"Oh I don't mind the Taffies and the Paddies, Alan. It's the
Muslims that I can't stand."

"So what have you got against Muslims?"

"The way they are taking over everywhere, building their stupid
mosques and starting wars all over the Middle East."

"So what is your religious faith, John? Is it Christianity" asked
Thelma.

"Yes."

"Are you proud of being a Christian, John?"

"Yes, I suppose I am."

"Well, can you tell me who started the First World War? Was it
the Muslims or the Christians? Second, who was it that started the
Second World War? Was it the Muslims or the Christians? And do
you know during those two wars, around half a million Muslim
soldiers fought in the trenches for the British Empire."

"I never knew that."

45

"And who was it that that dropped nuclear bombs on Hiroshima and Nagasaki and what religion were Hitler, Franco and Mussolini. I think that you will find they were all Christians."

"That was all in the past."

"Maybe it was, but its legacy carries on. You said that you didn't like the blacks in America. Who was it that took more than 12 million slaves out of Africa and on their sea journey to the New World over a million died or were thrown overboard?"

"Tell me who killed 20 million Aborigines in Australia? Who killed millions of native Indians in North and South America? It wasn't Muslims. It was something that Christians did."

"Where do you get all that information from? I've never heard any of that stuff before."

"You can get it on the internet if you know where to look."

"I don't have a computer."

"What paper do you read every day?"

"I don't read one. They all tell a load of lies."

"How much do you know about their religion of Islam?"

"Nothing, why should I?"

"How much do you know about Christianity and if you do know a little bit about it, can you tell me why it is split into at least a dozen different groups?"

"I didn't know that it was split into any different groups. Anyway, I am not that interested to be honest."

A little later, the conversation moved on to John talking about some of the places he had visited in America and some of the people he had met. As a young man, he had enjoyed the sport of boxing. Following on from what he had said earlier, it thus came as a big surprise to them all, when he said that while he had been in New York, he had briefly met one of his boyhood heroes.

It was the great Muhammad Ali, someone who was both black and a Muslim and maybe bizarrely, someone who John was very pleased and proud to have shaken hands and spent time with.

8. Pissaro, Picasso and Phil's uncle Jack

As they ate their evening meal, as she usually did, Thelma would tell Alan about any people she had met during the course of the day. And today she had something very interesting to tell him about a conversation she had had with Mrs Liptrot in ASDA.

"Do you remember last year, Channel 4 inviting the public to get involved in what it called its *Big Art Project*. The aim was to inspire local communities to create public works of art that would become lasting physical legacies."

"Yes. Something like that."

"And do you remember that St Helens Council put forward the site of the old Sutton Manor colliery, but it never got put onto the final short list."

"Yes."

"Well, Mrs Liptrot told me today that the Project's governing body, have now found that all those six sites, are facing problems. So they have decided to include Sutton Manor again. It was also because they were very impressed with the enthusiasm for it shown by that former miners' focus group."

Before she could say any more, the phone rang. It was Rebecca wanting to tell her mother the very same news and by the end of the day, it was all over Ashurst, hardly surprising as any such sculpture if constructed would be less than three miles from the centre of the town. And if it was as tall as some had said it might be, then it would be seen from all over Ashurst as well.

Whether it was discussed at work the following day, Alan would not know as he had to spend it at Fiddlers Ferry Power Station in the Control Room. He did not get back home until turned five and as he flopped on his chair, he told Thelma that he had had a very tiring day. Then he asked her what was for tea.

"I don't know."

"That's unlike you, knowing that I have been out all day grafting away at the coal face in order to put food on the table. Surely there are still a couple of slices of bread left in the pantry. Or did you have them for your dinner?"

"No, and we won't be eating anything here tonight either."

"How come. You said you still had a shilling in your purse last night."

"I had to put it in the electric meter this morning."

"Why didn't you put your overcoat on?"

"I don't have it any longer. I had to pawn it last week."

"Let's hope it's going to be a mild winter."

It was a clear signal to Alan that Thelma had got something organised. She usually did when she behaved in this way.

"We've been invited out for tea tonight. Have you forgotten?"

"No. I haven't forgotten. I just haven't remembered. Give us a clue. Which kind soul in Silkstone Street is going to feed us or are we going to have to go to that food bank in Edge Lane?"

"Knowing what goes on in your head, I think you might need 20 clues."

"Next door. Don't tell me, it's probably Janice inviting us to celebrate the anniversary of the death of Pablo Picasso or maybe the birth of Camille Pissaro and then wanting me and Phil to move more heavy furniture upstairs."

"No. It's nothing like that. It's her birthday today and besides us two, there will also be another guest, someone that she once went to school with in Oldham."

"And is this person a painter by any chance?"

"I don't know. All I know is that Janice said that you will find her very interesting because she has done something that you have been promising to do for as long as she has lived here, but never have done."

"And what is this thing that I haven't done yet?"

"Written a novel."

"So this woman is a bit of an intellectual then."

"Seems like it."

"An intellectual from Oldham. That must be a first."

"You tell that to Janice."

"And where is her novel set? In Oldham by any chance?"

"I don't know. In fact I hardly know anything about her and I don't think that Janice knows much about her either as she hasn't seen her for years. According to what she told me this morning, Betty has been living abroad for quite a long time and for the last three years she has been in Cairo. Anyway you'll meet her soon. We are expected there at seven which might give you some time to swot up about what you know about the Middle East."

"Well for a start, I do know where it is."

"On the other hand it might be better for you to keep quiet when we get there and then not be thought of as a fool when you open your mouth and remove all doubt."

"What time are we going?"

"Seven o'clock, but we had better go a bit early just to make sure we get a good seat."

Just as they were about to leave the house, the phone rang. It was Penri from Aberthaw apologising for ringing, but with questions he needed answering immediately. As a result it was another 10 minutes before Alan was able to leave the house. He walked into next door and saw the others sat round the table waiting for him. Thelma immediately turned to Betty and said: "This is my late husband."

The meal started with Betty making reference to all the paintings on the wall which gave Janice an opportunity to talk about Camille Pissaro, her favourite painter. Betty talked about her interest in the post-impressionist school and how she had once met David Hockney. Then Phil lowered the intellectual tone of the evening, by saying that his favourite painter was his late uncle Jack. He had painted the house for Phil and his first wife Cynthia just after they were married in 1976 and the paint was still stuck to all the walls and in little need of attention.

Just as they were finishing the meal, the phone rang. Phil went to answer it and then came back a few minutes later with some interesting news. It was from his sister Janet who had just heard that Channel Four's big project had decided that it was going to include the Sutton Manor site on its list of possible locations for its big project.

Janice then asked where Betty had been for the last 30 odd years. This provided her old friend with the opportunity to give them a quite fascinating account of that earlier part of her life.

"After I left school, I got a job at Ferranti's in Hollinwood. One day the boss walked into our office and asked if anybody could speak French. I said that I could and he said that two French engineers had just arrived and neither spoke much English. I went up to the manager's office to meet these two men. I then told the boss that I had spoken very little French since leaving school and would need to have a French dictionary to make sure whatever I said was correct. So he sent somebody out to buy one while I spent over an hour talking to these two men. By the time the dictionary arrived, it was time for dinner so we all went into the managers' restaurant. By the end of the day, all had gone very well and then Yves told the boss that they had to go to a cotton mill in Failsworth the next day and asked if I could go with them.

The result of all this was I got to know Yves very well. I could soon tell that he had taken quite a fancy to me and before they left, he gave me his telephone number and told me that if ever I was in Paris, I could stay at his place. A few weeks later I rang him, handed my notice in and went over there, and moved in with him. It was 1968 when France was on the brink of revolution and Yves was in one of the revolutionary groups. Our first date was bizarre to say the least. It was spent on the barricades battling against the CRS and then back to his bedroom. How romantic it all was, but the a few weeks later we both got arrested. The CRS were really brutal that day, well they were pretty brutal every day. I spent some time in hospital and when I came out, I went to where the group had their headquarters and one of his comrades told me that Yves had just disappeared.

No one had a clue where the CRS had taken him and that was the last I ever saw of him. I hung around with other members of the group that he was in. It was the Servir le Peuple people, a Maoist group. They were good comrades and looked after me really well but I decided then to get out of France with a guy in a lorry going up to Belgium and I came back home from there. There was always a chance that he might have contacted me, but he never did. I went back to Paris some time later to see if I could find him or any of his friends but saw none of them ever again."

Alan had always had a great interest in the history of France and particularly the French Resistance during the war. In his early twenties he had also talked to many older workmates who had been involved in that six year-long blot on history. There was Stan who had taken part in the liberation of the Belsen Concentration Camp, Charlie from Thatto Heath and a member of the Paratroopers, the Wiganer Mick who had served on HMS Dolphus, Billy who had been called up in January 1945 and had fought his way all across the Rhineland and Sam Holroyd, the Merchant Navy seaman with his tales of trips in the middle of the Arctic winter to supply the Russian base at Murmansk.

Alan also had quite an interest in the Middle East. This stemmed from tales he had heard from one of his neighbours, when he lived in Chisnall Avenue. Stan Tyrer had seen active service first in North

Africa and then along with around 800 other servicemen had been drafted into the British Palestine Police around early 1945.

And it was while he had been in his last year as an apprentice and on night shift in the Copper Refinery that Alan had also learned more about the Spanish Civil War. When everything was running smoothly, he had talked at length with and learned a lot from the electrician Jack Parr. Jack's brother Tommy had joined the International Brigade and been wounded in the battle of Jarama. On returning home to Ashurst, he had written about his experiences and what had happened to three other Ashurst lads who never came back.

Unfortunately he had not been able to put it into a state that would have been good enough to send to a publisher and then in the autumn of 1940, he had been killed in the first German bombing raid on Liverpool. Jack had inherited all Tommy's possessions and knowing of Alan's interest, had given them all to him to read and keep if he wanted them.

Around the time that he was based in the Electricians' Shop, Alan was very pally with a lad called Andy who had a couple of years earlier had been heavily involved in the Apprentices' Movement. Then right out of the blue, he had handed in his notice in and left. Alan knew nothing more about what had happened to him until over 12 years later, while he had been on a job at West Burton Power Station. Hearing a couple of men talking in the canteen one lunchtime, he was sure by the way one talked, that he came from Nook End.

At the time the Nook End accent was very distinctive. From his conversation with the man, Alan discovered that he was Andy's younger brother, Jack.

In this way, he learned what had happened to Andy and how he had changed so much. He had left Wilkinson's and Ashurst with the intention of joining an anarchist group based in Paris. He had hitched his way down to Dover aiming to take the ferry to Calais and was within a mile of the port when the car he was travelling in, had been in a crash. This had put Andy in hospital for the next two months. By the time he was ready to be discharged, he had fallen in love with one of the nurses and moved in with her in her cottage in a place nearby called Birchington.

From then on, Andy changed dramatically. He forgot about all his revolutionary ideas and began to regularly attend her local

51

church. He joined its choir and played for their flat green bowling club team. According to Jack, Andy also managed to do something that very few people from Nook End had ever done in their lives. He had managed to lose his Nook End accent.

Driving home later, Alan remembered another person who had done something similar. It was Pat Grantham, who on leaving Lane Head Junior School, had gone to Ashurst Girls Grammar School and then on to Oxford University where she had joined the Young Conservatives. At the age of 10 she was little different to all the other girls in their class, but 15 years later she appeared in a BBC2 television programme. There wasn't the slightest trace of an Ashurst accent in anything that she said. Money spent on her elocution lessons had clearly been well spent.

Back at work, the following day as they all began to eat their lunch, Jennifer said: "What did you do after you got home from Richard Burton's power station last night, Alan? Playing marbles in the road again, I bet."

"No. It was too dark for that when I got home and Rupert's mummy wouldn't let him play out with me because he had been a naughty boy because he had said a rude word to their new maid."

"So what did you do? I bet you were on the internet again."

Ever since Jennifer and her sister Mary had started producing *The Gap*, Alan had not only read it with great interest. He had also frequently discussed its contents with her during their lunch break. This had led him to spending more time on the internet at home, reading articles which opened up a completely new view about what was really going on in the world at large. But despite that level of interest, he still had difficulty understanding much of the material that appeared on his screen, which was one reason why he liked to talk to Jennifer about them so much.

"Thelma went up to Moss Bank to see her friend Joan so I decided to do a bit of investigation about things that matter."

"And what did you discover or did you just finish up registering for some online dating service with a bored French house wife who lives just 100 metres from your house, while Thelma was out of the house."

"No. I learned a lot more about how the Keynesian economic policies that had dominated world economy and trade, since the Wall Street crash, were failing the big multinational corporations by around 1970. This led them to look towards ideas that were based on deregulated banking systems, free trade agreements and the reduction of trade union power all in order to ensure they could continue to maximise their profits."

She nodded her head and said correct in a way that indicated that she wanted to hear him say more and so he continued: "I can now understand much more clearly how, ever since 1980, we have suffered a dogma driven mania for privatising everything in this country. We have been led to believe by the Tories, Liberals and by Tony Blair too and all his neo-liberal supporters that unleashing the power of the market and the private sector into the public services, would be more efficient and better value for money for everybody. Well, that never happened under Thatcher, it didn't happen under John Major and it certainly didn't happen under Laughing Boy either."

"And was Thelma pleased with all your investigations, when she got back home?"

"Not much. When she went into the kitchen, she saw that I hadn't done the washing up and I'd left the oven on."

"You see, Alan, what the supporters of neo-liberalism don't appreciate is the consequences for society of allowing the bankers to operate without any form of state or government control or regulation. They behave as though they were running a casino and it is all going to lead to a world crisis. One thing, for example, is the growth of unemployment. All those people who no longer have jobs, can no longer buy things, which means that the demand for goods falls and so profit cannot be made on them, which is the very basis on which our present economic system is based on."

Interesting times ahead no doubt, Alan thought as he drove home after work. Interesting yes, but also very worrying too for the younger generation and particularly for his three grandchildren Josh, Joanna and now little Daisy.

Little did he appreciate then that within less than two years, the world's whole monetary system would be on the point of complete collapse, caused by the greed and recklessness of a very small number of highly paid and socially irresponsible men and women all aided by an economic model that was almost certainly doomed to fail in the long run!

It wasn't worrying about the state of the world's economy though that made him ill for the next few days. It was probably some food poisoning since Thelma had suffered too and so he did not go back into work until the following Monday. Then during the lunch break he proceeded to tell Jennifer about what he had discovered while he had been away: "I decided to google in the name of Maynard Keynes to see what sort of a person he was. I was very surprised by what I found out about him."

"Like what."

"What I didn't know was that if the British Government had listened to him after the end of the First World War, the whole history of Europe and the world might have been totally different."

"I am intrigued. Carry on, professor."

"It turns out that he was a member of the British delegation to the Versailles Treaty meeting in Paris in 1919. His view was that if any treaty that was imposed on Germany was far beyond the ability of Germany to pay, it would ultimately lead to disaster but he was largely ignored. Germany was never able to pay those penalties and the resentment that treaty caused in Germany was one of the factors that led to the rise of Hitler and the Second World War."

Then Cliff chipped in to say that the conditions in this country had been pretty bad for most of the population of Britain too, but he agreed they were nowhere near as bad as they had been for the people in Germany. Moreover, he didn't know all that from reading history books or from going on the internet but from what had been told to him by members of his own family over the years.

He wasn't disagreeing with Alan though. That was something that rarely happened. It was just Cliff's way of recognising that it was a great pity that Keynes had not had much greater support from among more influential members of the British ruling class.

9. The Welsh Chambermaid

The days and weeks passed and soon they were well into March. Alan had not been needed at work for a few weeks now. In some ways it suited him to have this arrangement. He could always find plenty of things to do in the house and garden, plenty of people to visit and grandchildren to play with, as well as spending time on his computer, along with watching and talking about rugby league. Then, right out of the blue, Duffy asked him to return. Tariq had been off sick for the last fortnight, Shaun was spending even more of his time back at Drax Power Station and the boss needed Alan to come back to complete a job that he had started at Aberthaw just before Christmas but had never been able to finish. Now it had suddenly became top priority which meant that he would have to go down to South Wales in order to sort out what still had to be done in the coal handling plant.

He stayed three nights in a small hotel at Cowbridge, a few miles away. He went back to the power station on Friday morning, had one more discussion with the engineer, Penri, to clarify everything that they had discussed the previous day and then left. He drove up to Llantrisant, turned left onto the A4119 and headed towards the A470. Going this way meant that he could drive through Tonyrefail which was where Thelma had been born in 1944. As he slowly drove through it, he looked at its houses, shops and pubs and wondered what her life would have been like if her mother had not died when Thelma was still a baby. In the centre of the town he saw a smallish middle aged woman stood at a bus stop on the other side of the road carrying a large bag of shopping. She even looked a little bit like his wife.

For Alan it was like passing into another world or switching to a parallel universe. What sort of a life would Thelma have enjoyed if she had lived all her life in this small town? What might she have ever known or thought about Lancashire and its people? What would images of places like Ashurst, Leigh, St Helens and Wigan have meant to her? Would she have ever become a rugby league fan? Would she have ever married someone from a large family and then become the mother to two children and later the grandmother to two grandchildren, soon to be three? No one would or could ever know.

As he approached Pontypridd, he saw a young girl at the side of the road, thumbing a lift. He stopped and asked her where she was heading. Her reply came as a bit of a surprise to him.

"Blackpool. It's up north in Lancashire."

He told her to put her rucksack on the back seat and get in. Before he set off again, he noticed how cold she looked.

"You look frozen. Here, have a drink of this" and produced his flask of hot coffee.

She drank it slowly and so it was some time before she started to talk and tell him a bit about herself and why she was heading to the famous North West holiday resort.

He let her talk. He rarely did, whenever he was driving. 'I'm a bloke. I can only do one thing at a time' was his motto, not like Thelma who he reckoned could drive, talk, listen to music, look at a map and even do a bit of knitting too when she was driving. On the other hand, Marion reminded him of what his sister Joan had been like at her age which he thought must be about 18 or 19. But the sound of her accent reminded him greatly of his wife.

"Do you come from round here, Marion?"

"Not quite. I'm from Cardiff. It's a few miles away."

"You sound just like our Maud."

"That's an old fashioned name. Is it the name of your wife?"

"No. My wife's name is Thelma. Where I come from, men often refer to their wife as 'our Maud'. It's a bit like Londoners who might call their wife 'my trouble and strife' or 'her in doors'. It's a bit old fashioned really. The younger ones don't do that now so much, if at all."

"Where are you from, then?"

"South Lancashire. It's not really that far from where you are going. It's a town called Ashurst. I don't suppose you will have heard of it before."

"No, I haven't."

"It's near to St Helens and Wigan. Have you heard of those two towns?"

"I've heard of St Helens. Many years ago my great uncle played for their rugby club."

"What was his name?"

"George Parsons. I think he lived in Abertillery before he went north, although I never met him."

"I remember him well. He was one of my favourite players when

56

I first started watching the Saints. It would have been just after the war in the late 1940s."

Although she was not Welsh by birth, she really did have a very pleasing accent. She had been born in England in Chepstow which was just a few miles from the Welsh border. But at the age of five, both her parents had died and she had been taken to live with her late mother's sister in Barry, a few miles west of Cardiff.

"And do you still live there now?"

"Well, it's all a bit complicated. I did until last November when my auntie became ill and then she went to live in a home and the house had to be sold and I had to leave. Until yesterday I was sleeping on a sofa with some friends in Cardiff. In September I am going to Lancaster University, but until then I've got a job working as a chambermaid in a hotel in Blackpool. It's a live-in job and that's why I am heading there now."

Their conversation was halted when an idiot driver in front of them suddenly veered over to the left in front of them and then changed his mind and came back right in front of them.

"I hate driving sometimes, what with idiots like that around."

Silence reigned for a few minutes and then Alan said: "So are you moving into your new place tonight? Are they expecting you?"

"I don't know. The man who gave me the job has left and I can never get hold of whoever is now in charge, on the phone."

They drove on steadily. Marion stopped talking and suddenly Alan noticed that she had fallen asleep. She had a young face obviously, but she looked a little more than tired though not haggard. Maybe life had not been quite that good for her in view of what she had just told him.

An hour later, he pulled into the car park of a Little Chef and stopped the car with a jolt.

It woke Marion up who looked around and worryingly asked where they were.

"I don't really know" said Alan. "But I do know I am hungry and I guess you are too, so let's go and eat."

"Alan, I haven't got very much money. I don't think I will be able to afford it. The place looks quite expensive."

"Don't you worry about paying for it. Wilkinson's Engineering at 27 Mersey Street on Warrington Road in Ashurst are paying for both of us. Come on."

"You are very kind, Alan."

57

"I'm a Lancashire man."

"Will they all be as nice as you in Blackpool?"

"Good question."

Back in the car an hour later, Marion soon fell asleep again and before much longer they were crossing the Thelwall Viaduct. Alan knew that he would soon be back home in Ashurst, but then what to do with Marion? He couldn't really offer to drive her up to Blackpool. That was partly because he was knackered. He used to like driving but much less so now and certainly not long distance. Aberthaw to Ashurst was just about his limit, Aberthaw to Blackpool and then back to Ashurst was well over his limit.

But then even if he had taken her all the way up to Blackpool, there was no guarantee that there would be a place for her to move into straight away. More worryingly though, if he just dropped her off as he came off the M6, she would not have found it easy to get a lift at that time of night as well. So he made a suggestion that could have been fraught with danger for a young girl in these circumstances.

"Marion, I don't think that you will get to Blackpool tonight. And what happens if there is no room for you when you get there. Can I make a suggestion? I know that Thelma would love to meet you. How would you like to stay the night in our house? We've got a spare room and that way you can ring up the hotel in the morning and make sure they are ready for you."

"You really are very kind, Alan. Are you sure it will be all right?"

"Over the years quite a few people who have needed help, have slept in that back bedroom. Even Thelma did when I first met her and on Christmas Day too, back in 1962. She'll love to welcome you, particularly if you lay your Cardiff accent on a lot."

20 minutes later they were home in front of his house in Silkstone Street. They walked into the living room and found Thelma fast asleep in front of the TV.

"Mrs Greenall, have we got room for a nice Welsh lady for evening meal, supper, bed and breakfast. This is Marion who I have just brought up from near Tonyrefail of all places."

Thelma rubbed the sleep from her eyes and said:

"Of course she can. She looks all in. What's your name again?"

"Marion."

"Come on then, Marion. I'll take you to your room and show you where the bathroom is as well. I'll get you a towel too. You'll need

58

to have a shower if you have been sat in that car all day."

It was typical Thelma. Always keen to help somebody who needed a bit of help, just like she had needed some help herself on Christmas Day 1962 and in the same house too.

And so Marion did stay for the night and on Saturday night too and was able to make contact on the phone with the new manager of the hotel who said she could move in straight away.

During her time with the Greenalls, she talked a lot with Thelma, mainly about what Tonyrefail and Cardiff were like now. The home and the street in Tonyrefail where Thelma had once lived had been demolished some time ago but the soap works in Cardiff was still there although it was now a car showroom.

After they had finished their breakfast on the Sunday morning, Marion asked what was the best way for her to get to Blackpool.

"In our car. It will be a nice ride out for us and I don't think that Thelma has been to Blackpool before and if I let her drive, we'll probably be there in about 20 minutes."

The hotel Marion was about to start work in, looked quite a decent place when they arrived there. The first person she spoke to was the manager. As soon as he started talking, she was pleased to discover that he was also from South Wales, in his case Port Talbot. Alan and Thelma had come into the place with her and so he assumed they might be her parents.

"No, they aren't, but they are my guardian angels." Marion said to him.

"Well I'm glad you have arrived. The other two girls have not turned up yet and I haven't heard from them either so you can start first thing in the morning. You can also have the best room as well and they will have to share a room if and when they arrive."

Marion shook hands with Alan and gave him a little kiss on the cheek. She hugged Thelma, thanked the both yet again for all that they had done for her and promised that she would keep in touch. That might have been the end of it though, people often say they will keep in touch, but never do. It's not that people are bad or negative or anti-social. It's just how things often pan out in life. But shortly after they had eaten their evening meal on the Monday evening, there was a loud knock on the front door. Standing there in front of them was a policewoman.

"Sorry to disturb you" were her first words. "We are just checking up on an incident in Blackpool over the weekend."

She went on to explain that an old age pensioner had been robbed in a back street by a young woman on the Saturday night. She had given a description of her attacker to the police as had another witness. That morning the witness had seen what he was sure was the attacker coming out of a shop and going into a hotel. He had followed her into the place and then asked Reception to ring the police. When questioned, the 'suspect' had said that she had only arrived in the town on the Sunday lunchtime, but her alibi still had to be checked. It was clearly a case of mistaken identity as both the Greenalls were able to indicate.

It would have been a lot more difficult though for Marion to have proved her innocence if she had arrived in Blackpool after hitching a lift in anybody else's vehicle.

Helping Marion had made them miss the Challenge Cup game against Batley on Friday evening, but there was no way they would be missing the following Friday night's game. It was away against the old enemy from the other side of Billinge. Over 24,000 people were there and at the end of the game, the most happy ones in the crowd were those from the south side of Billinge.

After that game, which Saints won 32–14, the next two games were both at home. The first was against Salford which Saints won easily 48–4 and the second was against Catalans Dragons which the Red Vee again won easily 53–10.

Coming back home after the victory over the French team, Alan asked his next door neighbour: "What would you rather watch, Phil. Saints losing in a very tight match by two or three points or Saints winning like tonight by over 40 points."

"Well, I did think it was a bit flat tonight, but then any game has got to be pretty good to be better than that Wigan game."

"Well, I think I'll start that campaign of mine going again about changing the rules."

"What's that?"

"When a team has scored a try, why should they get the advantage of possession on the restart? It just helps one team get a roll on. They don't do that in soccer."

"What do you mean?"

"Say Liverpool are playing Bolton. Liverpool score a goal and so Bolton restart with possession on the halfway line. It would seem stupid if after scoring a goal, for Liverpool to get possession at the kick off."

60

"Fair point, I suppose. It's worth a try."

"Well that's my goal. I'll have to write to Nigel Wood about it."

"Have you ever met him, Alan?"

"I spoke to him once when he was at a RLSA meeting that I went to at Salford."

"Is their magazine *TGG* still going?"

"Yes. Issue number 53 arrived in the post last week. There's a piece in it about rugby league in Jamaica and an article called *European Development Going Dutch* that looks interesting. Do you know that it has been going since 1990? That's over 17 years, not bad I reckon even though it is always late arriving."

""My brother used to buy all the fanzines before he got married. There was *The Dark Satantic Mills* from Leigh, *The Loiner* from Leeds, *The Steam Pig* from Bradford, *Wally Lewis is Coming* from Wakefield and Salford's *The Scarlet Turkey* and two Saints ones, *The Director* and *Rahrt Up T' Tas*h. There was also one called *London Calling* as well."

"Well we do have a great history, Phil and I've just started reading that book *Rugby League in its own Words* again. It's written by two fans, one a Saint and one a Loiner. It's written as though rugby league was a real person. I think I told you about it when we were coming back from the Cup Final last year."

And then he continued: "Do you know that rugby league is the only sport that knows the exact date of its birth. Thursday 29 August 1895 in the George Hotel in Huddersfield."

"I do know that, Alan. You've already told me that about three times this year already."

Then he turned to Thelma who was sat in the back with Janice and said: "How many times has he told you, Thelma?"

"There's nothing wrong with him telling everybody that he meets, about that meeting in Huddersfield in 1895. Let's face it, he's the only man still alive who was there."

10. Callaghanism and neo-liberalism

"Good morning Jennifer. I expect that you will be pleased to hear that your old mate Mr Blair has gone?"

"Loose language is that, Cliff. For starters, he is no old mate of mine and he has not actually gone. He is just no longer the Labour Party leader. One thing is certain though, he'll soon be going round everywhere, giving long winded speeches and charging an extortionate fee for them as well, no doubt."

"And in your view, will this change be a good thing or a bad thing for the Labour Party?"

"When he took over after John Smith died, it had 400,000 members. That number is now down to around 190,000. In other words, New Labour policies and with him as the leader, have led to over half of its members leaving. That tells it all, I think."

"So, in your opinion, what was it that New Labour did that caused all these members to leave?"

"The most obvious thing was the invasion of Iraq with him ignoring international law about the use of armed force to bring about regime change. The other thing was with the NHS. At first it did get big increases in health care spending with big improvements being made in the quality of care and reduction in waiting times. But from around 1999 onwards, they started to change it from being a completely public sector provider to one that began to include private sector involvement.

At the same time, they moved from tolerating private enterprise to promoting it with all its market structures, Foundation Trusts, GP consortia, and the introduction of private finance corporations into commissioning in the NHS.

All this was in huge contrast to what was in their 1997 Manifesto which said that 'Our fundamental purpose is simple but hugely important: to restore the NHS as a public service, working co-operatively for patients, not as a commercial business driven by competition'.

That was what a lot of people had voted for and then they saw that they were not going to get it. Put more bluntly, they began to realise that they had been lied to."

She paused while Tariq interrupted them in order to tell Alan that he was going to collect his car from Canal Street garage.

After he had left, she continued: "The Labour Party was formed in 1906 as an organisation to serve the interests of the working class. I don't think it can still be said to do that now. For a start, an increasing number of their MPs have very little in common with the working class. Few of them have ever had what most ordinary folk would consider to be a proper job. They look, talk, dress and behave more like members of the establishment. In fact St Helens now has a millionaire as its Labour MP. Can you believe that, in a town like St Helens?"

"Frankly, no."

. "Do you think that Gordon Brown will be any different?"

"No. He'll carry on where Blair left off. Allyson Pollock, a professor of public health research at Bart's Hospital interviewed him recently. When she told him how critical she was of PFIs, he told her that the public sector was bad at management and that only the private sector was efficient and could manage services well. A socialist would never say something like that, would he?"

"No."

As she spoke, she was interrupted by John Carter who had just walked into the office. He was quite an abrasive character, a strong Labour Party supporter and, like its new leader, a Scot, although he had now lived in Huyton for over 10 years.

"So what's your tiny organisation going to do for the working class then, madam?"

Alan put down the manual he had been holding and said:

"John, Jennifer's organisation has just entered a coalition with the Greens, the Liberals, the SNP, Plaid Cymru, the NHS Action Party and the Gillarsfield Freedom Party to offer voters a credible alternative in opposition to the Labour lot and the Tories."

"Not like you to spoil the start of a good discussion."

"No, Cliff, but I've just remembered that Duffy is coming round here at half ten with some visitors, so much as I would like to talk about things much more interesting than block cable diagrams or panel assemblies, can you all try and tidy this place up a bit?"

True to form Mr Duffy did appear, although over an hour later with an engineer from Scottish Power. By that time Alan had also been rung from the sub-station in Birkenhead by Dave Morris. It meant that he would have to go there, first thing after lunch.

As soon as their visitors had left, Alan called the rest of them together and told them all to listen carefully.

"We have just won a big order from a company in Brazil so we need to finish all the jobs in the office by Monday. The other thing is that Dave Morris has found a problem on that job on the Wirral and I am having to go and sort it out this afternoon and tomorrow morning as well. So will you all be able to keep yourselves busy until I get back here in order to feed you at lunch time."

"Sounds as though you will be making a meal of it."

"Well I have got a lot on my plate, as you well know, Cliff."

"While you are away on the beach at New Brighton, when I want to go to the Ladies, who do I have to ask permission from?"

"You don't have to ask permission to go to the Ladies, Jennifer" said Cliff. "You can go there as often as you want. You only have to ask permission if you want to go to the Gents!"

An hour later Alan was driving through the Mersey Tunnel. He had been through it before but always as a passenger in somebody else's vehicle. Now he was there on his own and as he drove, his mind went back to his first visit. It was during the summer holidays probably in the early 1950s when he had been playing in the road with his mates John Harris and Geoff Platt and when John's Dad had walked over to them and said:

"I'm going to New Brighton in the van in half an hour. Do any of you want to come with me?"

All three said yes, but Geoff's mother would not let him go as she wanted him to run an errand for her. There was nothing special to recall about the journey from Chisnall Avenue to Liverpool. But as the van entered the tunnel, he had been very frightened by its dark surroundings and bright lights. It was just as bad on the return journey and he remembered how glad he was when the van was back in the centre of Liverpool.

The next time he was there was with Wilkinson's first and third rugby union teams going to play a club at Hoylake. Alan had made his first team debut that day and had even scored a try. In fact it was the only try scored that day but the home team still won. They were obviously a very traditional rugby union club and scored all their points, some 24 of them, all from goal-kicks.

Back in work the following day and before he even had switched on his computer Jennifer walked into his office.

"Bad news, boss. You know yesterday when you said that our little organisation had entered into a grand coalition for the next General Election with the Liberals, the Green Party, SNP, Plaid Cymru

64

and the Gillarsfield Freedom Party."

"Yes."

"Well the last lot had to put it to a referendum of all their members. Last night their National Secretary told me that the result of the voting was three for this grand coalition, two against and two abstentions. According to their constitution it falls, because every decision has to have a majority. So now I have to ring Nick Clegg and see if it makes much of a difference to him."

"So what's the problem?"

"I don't have his telephone number. Do you?"

Then she went all serious again and said: "I was on the phone for over an hour with our Mary last night. It's amazing what she can find out about. It must be something to do with her being five minutes older than me."

"Go on then. Tell me what she's told you this time."

"According to her, people are wrong if they think that neo-liberalism only surfaced in this country after 1979 when the Thatcher government took over. It wasn't. She believes that it began under the previous Labour Government when Denis Healey as Chancellor of the Exchequer had to apply to the IMF for a two and a half billion pound loan. For this, the IMF demanded that Britain moved away from its Keynesian methods of economic management, one which relied on high levels of public spending to sustain its welfare state, to one based on something called Monetarism, which would accept higher levels of unemployment along with a greatly reduced role for the state.

As a result, Callaghan's government had to agree to reduce its public expenditure and explains why since then, there has been an ever-decreasing proportion of our GDP being spent on such things as the NHS, Education, Social Services along with a growing demolition of many publicly owned industries and all driven by the free market dogma of 'private sector good: public sector bad'.

This was also when finance capital began to replace manufacturing capital as the basis for the accumulation of wealth. It will all be in an article she is writing for the next issue of *The Gap*. She might well call it something like 'Callaghanism and the creation of more wealth for the few by the many'."

"And in her view will neo liberalism in this country be affected by this country now having a government led by Gordon Brown?"

"No, he's wedded to the free market economy just like Blair was before him and like many of his right wing MPs still are as well. Its main selling points are that free markets are best at allocating resources and that government intervention and regulations on business should be kept to an absolute minimum along with a big reduction in all trade union power and influence."

As Alan walked back in to his office, his train of thought about the way the world economy was heading, was interrupted by a phone call to tell him that Mrs Thatcher had just arrived and was now waiting in Reception with her.

"Eunice, what is today's date. Is it April the First?"

"I knew you would say that Alan, but this Mrs Thatcher is not that Mrs Thatcher. She's good looking for a start. She knows how to smile at you and she looks as though she means it."

Then he remembered that he had arranged for a sales rep from Foster's Electrical to visit him, someone with a not very popular surname with which to travel round parts of the industrial north.

She had a selection of literature providing information about her company's wide range of electrical products and told him that although the company was based fairly close to Sunderland's new football ground they were aiming to open up a depot in Runcorn.

"You won't impress me by talking about football grounds. You are in rugby league land round here, but you might impress me by saying you have a Sunderland connection."

"Why is that?"

"Because one of our engineers comes from near Sunderland and is an expert on tariff metering and a nice young lady as well."

"Well, I can't say that I am very impressed. I am a Newcastle United fan and we hate the Mackems."

"It's like that round here. There's great rivalry between St Helens and Wigan fans and some people from both towns say they hate the other, but to be honest most don't. It's just a few idiots on both sides who say that and mean it."

"Alan, I don't know how you can ever enjoy watching rugby."

"Well Janet, I bet that you didn't know that there are two versions of rugby. What you have probably seen on your TV and been utterly bored by, is rugby union. What we play round here is rugby league. In fact there's also a team that now plays at that big athletics stadium in Gateshead."

"Thanks for telling me that but I'll never go there. I can't stand grounds like that one. You are too far away from the players and there's no atmosphere. Not like at St James Park. Although again I don't like having to sit down, I'd much rather stand up and shout."

"You shouting! You do surprise me."

"Anyway I had better be off now. I've got to visit a firm in Blackburn. Do they play your sort of rugby round there?"

"No. I'm afraid it's all football up there as well but I'll tell you what I'll do for you. Next time you come, I'll get you a DVD of one of the greatest rugby league games that you will ever see. It's between my team, the Saints and the Bradford Bulls and it had one of the most dramatic ends ever. We call it the "Wide to West" game and by then I hope I'll be in a position to place an order with you for some of this control gear you have just shown us."

11. "Was the Archbishop wrong?"

It was 10 o'clock and all the technical staff had now been sitting patiently in the meeting room for over half an hour. Why they had been told to attend was not known. It might possibly be to be informed that Amsterdam had finally decided to close the place down.

Usually when they were all waiting for Duffy to appear, they would find something more interesting than work to talk about and today it began with Tariq asking Alan if he knew what was happening with that Channel Four project at Sutton Manor.

"You remember in July, the Steering Committee chose the Catalan artist Jaume Plensa to mastermind the whole project. A few weeks ago he showed them his proposal. It was for a 20 metre high monument in the shape of a miner's lamp, which he had suggested calling *The Miners' Soul*. Surprisingly the committee rejected it, even though the majority of them had once worked there. They wanted something more modern day and progressive and so they asked Jaume to go back to Spain to design something more in line with their comments."

Alan's description of something that in two years time might dominate the landscape and be seen by thousands of drivers every day on the M62, elicited no further interest or discussion and so Alan went on to make one of his favourite suggestions:

"Why don't we all play *I Spy with my little eye*."

"That might be suitable for old age pensioners, but not for me."

"So what do you suggest we do, Cliff?"

"We could play *Are you the man who?* said Colin.

"That's sexist" said Jennifer.

"What's sexy about it?"

Now it was Tariq's turn to contribute to what was going to be a quite meaningless, though almost certainly humorous discussion.

"What she means, Tariq is that it is a game that misses out half the population of the world. The game *Are you the man who?* ignores the existence of women in the world."

"So what do you suggest we play, to pass away the time?"

"How about playing *Are you the woman who?* and I'll go first"

"Nice one Jennifer. I could see that coming."

"Let's discuss the situation in the Middle East" said Shaun.

68

"I'd rather discuss the situation in the Wild West." said Colin.

"I bet you would rather play Cowboys and Indians as well."

At this point they were joined by Dave Morris and Tony Griffiths, both installation engineers who spent most of their time working on jobs based all over the world.

"No Duffy here must means that the meeting is over. Looks as though we have just come at the right time."

"Have you just flown in from Schipol Airport, Tony?"

"No. I've just walked it from Warrington. Why?"

"It doesn't matter. Have you come for this meeting?"

"No. I've come to see Father Christmas. Don't tell me that he's got the sack."

"So, how is life in Stockton Heath these days?"

"It starts at 12 and it finishes at 12. What more can I say."

"You could say that it starts in bed and finishes in bed, which could be quite interesting."

"Depends who you are in bed with."

"Exactly. So who were you in bed with last night?"

"I don't know. I never asked her for her name. Cheeky little madam she was though. Woke up before I did, left and never even paid me."

"And how are things over in darkest Yorkshire, Dave?"

"Well it's certainly dark in the middle of the night."

"How's Elmer?"

Dave had a sister called Maureen who lived in London with her American partner John and Elmer was John's father. In the 1950s, Elmer had spent time as a GI at the nearby American airbase at Burtonwood. Alan had met him three years ago and had taken him to watch his first live game of rugby league at Knowsley Road against Wakefield Trinity.

"He's back in Italy now. Not doing too badly for a man of 82 from what I've heard."

"And what is happening in Hebden Bridge? Is your lass still selling all them second hand stones that you keep digging out of your back garden?"

A few years earlier, while working in the south of Italy, Dave had visited the ancient city of Pompei. On returning home he had put the word around that he had brought back some rare stones which, when boiled in a mixture of balsamic vinegar and sugared water, aided male performance. But after three years, none of the locals

69

could claim any benefit from this unusual concoction.

"So if you can tell us summat funny, you can have the floor until Duffy turns up."

Dave looked all around him and said:

"No thanks. I've got a better floor than this at home and I'd have nowhere to put it."

At this point Duffy's secretary reappeared: "Dave. There's a call for you on my phone."

"Toodoloo shipmates. See you all in Casablanca."

After he had left Alan said: "Can I suggest that we play *I spy with my little eye* again. Or maybe Jennifer can explain to us earthly mortals what is happening in the world of high finance."

"I can, on one condition."

"What's that?"

"You've got a job number for it."

"I'll find one. Go on then. Tell us."

""Well, the World Bank have now issued a statement predicting that global economic growth will slow down during the course of this coming year as this credit crunch, that I have been telling you about, begins to hit all the richest countries in the world."

At this point Duffy's secretary reappeared to tell them their boss would not be in work today and suggested they all carried on with what they had been doing the previous day.

They all returned to their computers and started work on it or returned calls to those who had rung while they were otherwise engaged in something of a fruitless exercise. But before Alan could even sit down, into the office came Horace.

"So what brings you here then Horace, it's only Thursday."

"I've got your new timesheets. You might need some time to understand how to fill them in."

"Does that mean that we'll also need a job number for working out how to fill them in? Have you brought one with you?"

Before he could answer, Alan's phone went and by the time he had returned, Horace had left. Nothing much worthy of note occurred that day and so it was later that evening when Thelma began to tell him about a couple of people who had been in the Oxfam shop that afternoon. But before she could get to anything interesting, their son Robert appeared. Megan and Daisy had gone to Wrexham, which was a good enough excuse for him not having to go home and make his own tea.

"Guess who I saw last week in the Co-op, mum?"

"Who?"

"Roger Wood. He was in our class for the final year."

"I remember him. What's he doing now?"

"He went to Bradford College for four years, qualified as a teacher and went to work at some right posh school in Cheshire."

"Has he changed much?"

"After you hear what he told me, you will see that he hasn't."

"Go on. Tell us. If it involves him, it's bound to be good."

"At the start of his second year there, a new headmaster arrived. He was a bit of a religious freak and one of the first things he did was to arrange for a series of talks to be given to the fifth and sixth forms on the role of religion in the world today. His first speaker was a Catholic priest who had just returned from Africa where he had been virtually cut off from the real world for years. When he heard about this, what Roger did, was to devise a cunning plan with a few rebellious members of the sixth form.

The priest gave a very traditional talk about his religion. Then the Head Boy, who was chairing the event, asked for questions from the audience but it was for three questions at a time so that they did not all get bogged down on any one issue. What few members of the rest of the audience knew was that Roger had arranged for some very embarrassing questions to be asked, with the first one being about the Vietnam War: 'During those terrible times, American planes dropped napalm on unarmed women, children and defenceless villages. After the pilots had returned to their base, if any of them had been Catholics and gone to Confession, would they have been expected to ask for forgiveness for committing such a terrible sin?'

The next question was asked by a boy whose uncle had suffered regular beatings at school by nuns, when he was only seven years old: 'Birth control is considered by your Church to be a mortal sin. One of my neighbours has a barber's shop at the bottom of our street. In his window, like most barbers do, he has an illuminated sign advertising Durex contraceptives. Do you think that is sinful and should he at least turn its light off on a Sunday?'

The third member of the gang then asked his question: 'Christianity believes that the Earth is around 6,000 years old. This is based on an analysis of the Bible done by one Archbishop James Ussher of Ireland, way back in the 17th century.

A hundred years later, James Hutton, the founder of modern geology, came to the well-founded conclusion that the history of the Earth could best be determined by understanding the processes of erosion and sedimentation. With his careful study of the formation of rocks, he showed that the Earth was more likely to be over four billion years old. Was he correct and if he was correct, does this mean that your Archbishop got it all wrong?"

Before Robert could tell them how the priest had reacted to these questions, Megan and Daisy arrived and more earthly matters had to be dealt with. Nothing more was said about Roger then and it was over a year later that Robert heard that his old friend was no longer working as a teacher and was now living with a teacher in Llandudno.

Soon after Megan and Robert had left, there was a knock on the front door. It was their next door neighbours, Janice and Phil, who had just returned from their visit to Spain where they were considering buying a house near the town of Calasparra in Murcia.

"We've got some bad news for you two" was the way the conversation was started by Janice. Alan and Thelma immediately feared the worst – that they were leaving.

"We are going to live out there, but only when the weather is really bad here."

"Well I am sorry to hear that. We were just getting to like you a little bit." said Thelma

"That's the bad bit. The good bit is that you can both come over whenever you want to."

"That's very nice of you. Any chance it could be just after the Grand Final in October?" said Alan

"You can't come over that soon because we have not even bought the place yet. And we haven't bought the place yet because it hasn't been built yet. And it hasn't been built yet because we haven't decided exactly where we want our little plot of land it will be built on, to be, and it certainly won't be before Phil's niece gets married."

"And when do you think that might be, Janice?"

"Don't know. She hasn't even started play school yet."

The following day around 11 o'clock Mr Duffy walked in with a visitor, a National Power engineer from Didcot Power Station. As soon as he opened his mouth, it was clear that the man came from the North East. He stayed for an hour, turned down Alan's

72

suggestion that they had lunch in Martindale's chip shop and left.

As soon as he had gone, Cliff said to Alan: "I think that fellow sounded like Mick Fleming who used to work in the Wiring Shop. Do you remember him? Big Saints fan, sounded like Jimmy Nail and looked a bit like Johnny Vegas."

"No" said Alan. "That man was nowhere near as broad as Mick. He sounded almost cultured."

"He must be from Sunderland then" laughed Cliff. "That's right, isn't it, Jennifer?"

Before she could begin to explain the difference in speech patterns between Geordies and Mackems, Alan went on: "I know who he did sound like, that Labour MP Alan Milburn. Where was he from Jennifer? It's somewhere up your way as well, isn't it. What do you know about him?"

"Quite a bit. In 2002 when he was the Secretary of State for Health he introduced NHS Foundation Trusts. They had more managerial and financial freedom than NHS Trusts which preceded them had ever had. They were a sort of halfway house between the public and private sectors and their introduction represented a big change in the history of the NHS and the way in which hospital services were managed and provided.

Later though he resigned from that position, citing difficulties combining family life up North with this job in London. But soon after, he became an advisor to Bridgeport Capital for 30 grand a year and still kept his job and his salary as an MP."

"What do Bridgeport Capital do? Do they build bridges?"

"Oh, nothing as useful as that. They are a venture capital firm, heavily involved in financing private health care companies that are hoping to move into the NHS."

"And you say that he kept his job as an MP as well. I'm surprised he would have found the time to do both."

"Oh, he would have found the time all right. People like him don't go into the House of Commons every day, you know. Many of these MPs have other jobs, some are inside the Palace of Westminster and some elsewhere in the City and further afield.

Milburn remained a backbench MP for a while, and then Blair brought him back into the government in 2004 and made him the Chancellor of the Duchy of Lancaster. I've now heard that he has also become an advisor to Pepsi Cola, for which he will get paid £25,000 a year to attend a handful of meetings and offer advice on

73

health and nutrition and various other matters."

"Sounds as though his rise to fame and a small fortune would make an interesting article for *The Gap*."

"That's the sort of an article that Mary would like to write, but she is far too busy at the moment, getting involved herself in something that could completely help transform British politics."

"What is it, another gunpowder plot?"

"No. It's something to do with the way that real news is made available through the internet to the public."

"A bit more than another newspaper, I take it."

"Mary has got to know a couple of women who are working on some plan to build a website that would cover the news that the mainstream papers either ignore or misrepresent. I don't think that the establishment will like it if it happens so she's told me no more about it."

"Well she does right. The British state has got its spies all over the place. In fact I was once told by somebody in the know that Special Branch were keeping tabs on Harold Wilson, even when he was the Prime Minister.

In fact I can also tell you a story a mate of mine told me about when he was working at Mount Pleasant Post Office in North London. It was quite near to where the *Daily Worker* used to be printed on Farringdon Road. Every night a couple of men came to one of the offices to look at some of the mail. One night my mate asked one of the older guys who had been there for years who were these people, as it was not always the same two.

'It's Special Branch just opening a load of letters to find out what some subversives are up to' was the guy's reply.

I also remember my mate Ray telling me that one day he received two letters through the post. One was from his brother who lived in Carlisle. Ray knew that because he could tell their kid's handwriting a mile off. But when he opened it up there was a typed letter from someone that he knew in Dundee. And when he open the letter which had the Dundee postmark on it, the letter inside was from his brother."

"You've not mentioned him for a bit. What is he doing now?"

"He'll be up to something. He always is. I am going to see him next week so I'll take him a copy of the latest issue of *The Gap*. It will be interesting to see what he thinks of it. In fact I bet that he might well want to start writing articles for it."

"Another writer for *The Gap* then and on top of that we've got a couple of new members in our readers' group. One is a junior doctor at Wrightington Hospital. He is probably a bit like Ray, forever ferreting out stuff about all the privatising and outsourcing that is going on behind the scenes in the NHS in the North West.

The other is a young lad who is a mechanic in a garage in Ashton. His dad and grandad were both active in the miners' strike and his uncle was heavily involved with Ricky Tomlinson and Des Warren in that Building Workers' Strike in 1972. They all seem to have left their mark on young Phil."

"When is your Mary coming up north again? Pity that the season has just finished as it sounds as though she could do with a bit of relaxation watching the Saints. Pity that she couldn't have come up last week as we could have taken her to Old Trafford watch the Grand Final."

Soon after, they all left work and went their separate ways. In Alan's case it was to the dentist's. But by half past five he was back home, ready and able to munch his way through his tea. As he ate it, he told Thelma how amazed he was at how many of his workmates and friends now had false teeth. Then he told her how his mother had always insisted that he cleaned his teeth every day after each meal whenever it was possible to do so and always without fail last thing at night. It had been exactly the same with his brother Paul and sister Joan. Both were older than he was, but perhaps most significantly and just like him, neither of them had ever smoked.

12. The Ashurst Poetry Group

"Has anybody here got any news
Or have we all just come for the booze
Now that our numbers are down to seven
Does that mean another old pal has gone to Heaven?"
"Has Greeno started reading the *Guardian?*"
"I assume by that, you mean the *Warrington Guardian*?"
There were seven former Wilkinson's employees sat in the Grange Social Club for their monthly get together. Some of the time, they would discuss what was going on in the world, other times one of them would ask for some help that one of the others could provide and sometimes they would spend the time having a go at one of those present. Usually it was Alan who suffered the most. But then it always had been that way, and today it was Pete Mulholland who was the first to reply to Alan's poetic offering.

"That would be a bit more correct if it said this:
'*Has anybody here got any news*
Or have we all just come for the booze
Now that our numbers are down to seven
Does that mean that another old pal has gone to Hell?'"
"Pete, you are numerically incorrect."
It was Len Jackson, a man well known for the absolute accuracy of anything he ever said or drawn.

"Ken Rainford and Keith Sanderson are in the bar so I am afraid your little ditty doesn't rhyme."
"How about this, then" chipped in Jack Shufflebottom.
"Has anybody here got any news
Or have we all just come for the booze
Now that our numbers are up to nine
Should we now all start drinking wine?"
"Pathetic. I didn't like poetry when I was at school and I don't like it now."
"So what did you like at school, Ronnie?"
"Music."
"Music. You? Never."
"Which instrument, Ronnie?"
"The dinner bell."
At this point Ken and Keith walked towards them and as they sat

down, John Mather said: "Keith, when you were at school did you like poetry?"

"No. Why."

"Bad news for you then. They are going to turn this group into the Ashurst Poetry Group. And the chief bard is going to be your old shirk mate, Horatio Greenall."

"He's not Welsh is he?"

"No, but their Thelma still is."

Then Ken said that he had always liked poetry and could remember a poem he had first heard around the time he had first started work in Wilkinson's Drawing Office back in 1966.

"Go on. Tell us as long as it has only got four lines."

"It was after the Saints beat Wigan at Wembley. Alex Murphy wrote it and sent it in a telegram to Central Park for them all to enjoy. It went like this:

'*Roses are red*
Violets are blue
St Helens Twenty One
Wigan Two'"

Then he carried on: "Do you remember Barry Littler from Billinge going working at a firm somewhere down south and every year when they got a pay increase, everybody had to send the MD a thank you letter. That was not something that Barry had ever done before and he wasn't very happy there either so he wrote something like this:

'*Roses are red*
Violets are blue
How do you expect me?
To manage every week on
Fifteen pounds nine and two.'"

At this point another old timer shuffled in. It was Ken Platt, often likened to the famous comedian with had once worked as a cable drum pusher at the Anchor Cable Works in Leigh.

"We are up to double figures now." said Shuffy. "I wonder what rhymes with 10. Have you got any news from the outside world, Ken? If not I am going to declare this meeting dead and buried."

"Well I can tell you about someone who is dead and buried. Joe Smith passed away last week. His daughter told me this morning while I was waiting for the bus."

Not many of them remembered Joe because he hadn't worked

77

there long, but John did: "I remember him fairly well because a month after I started going out with his sister, he went to live with Red Ruth."

"Not quite right there, John. He went living in Redruth. It's a town down in Devon."

"Cornwall."

"Devon."

"Down south."

"I wonder if he liked it while he was there. Stan Middlehurst went to live down south near Eastbourne, didn't stay long and now he's come back up here and living in Vincent Street" said Alan.

"Living in Vincent Street with a woman from Parr, I believe. That's what Jack West told me in the Post Office yesterday."

"What's Jack doing now, Pete? The last time I saw him he was in a bookies on Wallgate in Wigan."

"Knowing what Jack was like when he was living in Nook End, probably the three Bs: Betting, Boozing and Billiards."

"Probably the Four Bs, more like as not. Betting, Boozing, Billiards and Brothels."

"There's no brothels in Nook End, are there, Keith?"

"Have you never been down Edge Street after eight o'clock, Stan?"

"Is that what time they open? Well I didn't know that."

Then Keith asked if any of them could remember Charlie Eccleston and his fascination, even obsession, with coincidences. Before any of them could say they did, he continued: "I went to see my cousin last week in hospital over in Halifax. When he was a young man he was a keen speedway fan and used to watch them play at Odsal every week. He was there one night sometime in the 1950s when one of the Bradford riders was in an accident from which he later died. On the same night there was another speedway meeting on at Norwich and again one of the riders was killed. So that was a bit of a coincidence in itself, because not many riders ever died in the course of a season, plenty of injuries, but few were fatal. The bigger coincidence was that both riders came from Burnley and the even bigger coincidence was that they had both once lived in the same street."

It was an interesting little tale but did not lead to anything else being said about it and soon after Ronnie stood up and said: "I am going home now but I have to say that I have thoroughly enjoyed

78

myself and have decided to come again. I take it you have these annual events every five years or more."

Soon after they all left and as they walked into the car park, they saw Len stood blowing into a police breathalyser. He never drank more than two pints which might hopefully mean that he was under the limit. If he wasn't then he would not be with them next month as it would not be that easy for him to get there from Rainford.

"So what earth shattering things did you talk about today?" asked Thelma as Alan bounced down onto the settee.

"The main item on the agenda was poetry."

He then asked her if she had a favourite poet. Her answer came as no surprise: "I am a Welsh lady and my favourite poet is Scottish."

"Don't tell me. Let me guess. It's William McGonigall.
'*Oh silvery bridge*
O'er the River Tay
Alas I am very sorry to say
That sixty lives were taken away
On the last day of 1869
Which will be remembered for a very long time'
I bet you didn't know McGonigall was a big rugby league fan."

"How do you know that?"

"Because he once wrote a poem called *A Tribute to Mr Murphy and the Blue Ribbon Army*. The first verse went like this:
'All hail to Mr Murphy, he is a hero brave
That has crossed the mighty Atlantic wave
For what purpose let me pause and think -
I answer, to warn the people not to taste strong drink.'"

"I reckon that he should have called it *A Tribute to Mr Murphy and the Red Vee Army*.
And then it could go something like this:
'All hail to Mr Murphy, he is a hero brave
That has crossed the mighty Irish Sea
For what purpose let me pause and think
To advice people to drink Greenalls
If they want a tasty strong drink.'"

Then Alan told her about something that Keith had told them about his daughter who was now a professor at Exeter University and which John had described as being "like tea from China".

Thelma laughed out loud and said: "That was one of Granny's

79

old sayings. I haven't heard anybody say that for such a long time. She had such a lot of them. She really did."

Then she continued with tales that she could remember from her early days living with his grandparents in 1963. Alan knew that when she said something like this, it was almost as though she moved into some form of spiritual contact with an old lady who had done so much for her in the now long distant past.

"Quite often if she had made a scouse or a hotpot or lobbies, for our dinner, she would serve Grandad from the pan first but with just one large spoonful. Then she would put plenty on my plate, then plenty on her plate and Grandad would look at his plate and say: 'That won't go far' and Granny would reply 'Put it on a number 24 bus and it'll go as far as Sutton Manor'. Then he would put his hand in front of his face, move his fingers towards him and say 'Come on, come on. We used to get more than that from Fritz, obviously referring to the four years of his life that had been wasted in that German prison camp.

They were really funny. They really were. Whether it was all for my benefit or not, I was never sure but I loved just listening to them talk and often it was the same story or the same bit of nonsense, but I just loved it.

If Grandad had gone out somewhere, the two of us might spend all afternoon talking, sat in front of the fire in the kitchen. Then when he came down the yard and into the house, the first thing that he would say would be something like 'Can I have a bit of that fire'. Then Granny would say 'Put big light on Ned first, and then we can see where you've been all day'.

When she had poured a drink of tea out for the three of us and he was in the yard or in another room and didn't come for it straight away, she would shout out: 'Ned, this drink is goin' be stone plonk if you don't come for it now.'

Sometimes she would say something was mint imperial. It took me a long time to realise what she really meant to say was it was immaterial and another one was 'Ee, I can't get out of me own road this morning. I'm in me Armorites'."

But before she could remind him that the Armorites were an ancient Egyptian tribe, the phone went again, she answered it, and then started on another of her marathon conversations with their daughter Rebecca.

Later that evening his neighbour Phil came round, wanting to

80

borrow Alan's electric drill. He was back 10 minutes later. The drill really was only needed for a five minute job. Then Phil said: "I'm sorry to hear that they didn't give you the job, Alan."

"What job? I already have a job. I've had it since 1962 if you hadn't noticed and not being a greedy person, one job is more than enough for me."

"It was the job of chief executive of the Rugby Football League. It's gone to Nigel Wood. Didn't you know? I was sure that you were favourite for the position and you are so modest too. You never even mentioned you were on the short list."

"So if Big Nigel has got the job what is going to happen to Richard Lewis? I hope he stays on. I know he has had his critics but then there's nobody in rugby league who hasn't had their critics and he certainly is keen to expand the game a lot more on an international scale."

Before Phil could reply, his partner Janice came into the house to tell him he was wanted on the phone and little more could be said about the matter as Thelma then came back into the room to tell Alan that he was now wanted on her mobile.

It was Jack Ashley, another former Wilkinson's apprentice who Alan had once known well. Jack had emigrated to Australia three years after coming out of his time. The next thing that anything was heard about him was in 1996 when he had moved to Athens to live with his son and his son's family. Now he was back in Ashurst and the reason for his call was to invite Alan and Thelma to meet Agnes, someone who he had recently got to know on his journey back home to Ashurst from Athens.

That might have sounded quite romantic if it had occurred on the road between the centre of the Greek capital and the airport at Eleutherios Venizelos. But it was on the train from Salford Crescent to Wigan Wallgate that they had met. It had been sparked off by Agnes seeing the Greek letters written on Jack's suitcase. She had casually mentioned to him that she had lived in Athens for a short while, a year ago. By the time she got off at Atherton, she had given Jack her telephone number and not long after she had moved in with him.

What Jack wanted to talk to Alan about was to ask him if he knew anything about a rumour going round the town about a proposal to build an incineration plant on the land in Mather Lane on which the former Victoria Nurses' Home had once stood.

The following day Jack rang again, this time inviting Alan and Thelma to come to a meeting to discuss hopefully help start a campaign going against its construction.

When they arrived at Jack's house a few days later there were 10 other people sat there in her front room. Jack began by suggesting that Agnes should chair the meeting. Her sister Maureen worked for the NHS in Manchester and knew a lot about what was happening behind the scenes. The sale of former hospital land was one of a number of things that were being negotiated well away from the public eye, all part, it would seem, of some great plan, to reduce the size and the role of the National Health Service right across the North West of England.

The meeting was quite useful for getting the campaign started and as they were discussing the date for the next meeting, Alan asked if he could bring his friend Ray Hewitt along. That was because he was also keen to get involved in any protests against the growing privatisation of the NHS, currently being organised by forces within the Labour Government.

"Is that the Ray Hewitt who used to go to Carlton Road Junior School and lives in Rivington Lane now?" asked a woman called Fay who had said hardly anything during the meeting.

"Yes it is. Why?"

"He was the first boy that I ever went out with. I often wondered what happened to him."

"Come to the next meeting and if he turns up, you'll see just how little or how much he has changed since then."

"I hope he has changed a bit since then. I hope that he has changed a lot since then. The last time I went out with him, his idea of a date was to take me trainspotting at Sutton Oak railway sheds."

13. New Year's Eve 2007

Thelma and Joanna were sat together in the living room. She and her brother Josh were staying the night at Granma's because their parents were going to a party in Penketh that evening. After spending the last hour preparing the food for tomorrow's meal, Thelma was now ready to spend time with Joanna who had been busy doing a jigsaw in the sitting room.

"What would you like to do now, Joanna?"

"Can you show me the family tree again please, Granma?"

"All right then. I'll go and get it from upstairs while you make some room on the big table."

The Greenall family tree was something that Alan had first started work on, during the winter of 1962 to 1963. Joanna had seen it for the first time a few days ago and not quite understood what it all meant. Or maybe she had understood what it all meant and was a little puzzled or even upset by one particular part of it.

A few minutes later Thelma reappeared and put two large sheets of paper on the table. She drew up a chair for Joanna to kneel on and told her that what was written in each box on the sheets was the name of a different member of the family. Then she pointed to a box at the bottom of the first sheet and said:

"Let's start with this one. Who do you think this person is?"

Joanna put her finger on the letters, mouthed them one by one and said: "It's says Joanna. Is it me?"

It was.

Thelma then pointed to the box next to it: "Do you know who this is?"

Joanna did the same again and then said: "It's says 'Josh'. He's my brother."

Then Thelma pointed to the lines going up from each box and on to a horizontal line that joined two more boxes together.

"The name in this box is Neil Rigby. Do you know who that is?"

Joanna looked at her and said: "I think it's my daddy."

"Very good, and who is this?"

In it was the name Rebecca Greenall.

Joanna was not quite sure and asked: "Is it my mummy?"

Thelma explained it was. Greenall was her mother's surname before she had got married and changed it to Rigby.

83

Thelma then pointed to a box a little higher up on the paper.

Joanna slowly mouthed the letters and said: "It's Grandad."

Then she smiled at her grandmother and said: "I like Grandad. He's always making me laugh."

Thelma smiled back at her and then pointed to the box which was joined to it by a short line.

"In this box is written the name Thelma Johnson. Do you know who that person is?"

Joanna put two fingers over her mouth and looked up at Granma and said nothing.

"It's me. That was my name before I got married to Grandad. That's when it was changed to Greenall."

Joanna smiled as she was now beginning to understand things a lot more clearly.

Thelma pointed to another box and again asked who it was.

Joanna traced her finger over the letters and said: "Is it uncle Robert?"

"Very good. So can you now see that a line going down means that goes to those relatives who were born to those who are above them? And a line going up is to someone who was born earlier, their mummy or their daddy for example".

Joanna looked into her grandmother's face and with a big smile, an indication that she was beginning to understand it all.

"Now, can you see this line going up from Grandad's name? It is going to a line that goes across to these two boxes. In them are Grandad's mummy and daddy. Grandad's mummy was called Isabella Doreen Holding. That was her name before she got married to Grandad's daddy. His name was Frank Arthur Greenall."

She looked into Joanna's face. It was bright and shining, now that the family tree was becoming a lot easier to understand, well almost.

"Going up from Doreen Holding are the names of her mummy and her daddy. They are also Grandad's grandparents. The name of his grandad was Albert Edward Holding and the name of his grandmother was Mary Isabella Tabern. That was before she got married to his Grandad. Do you understand it all so far, Joanna?"

Joanna nodded keenly.

"Let's call this sheet, Number One sheet. At the top of it, are all the names of lots of relatives in the family going back in time, all starting with Grandad's grandmother."

Then she moved across to the other sheet and said: "Let's call this sheet, Number Two sheet."

Then she pointed to the box with Grandad's name in it again and said:

"On this sheet we have the names of lots of relatives going back in time, starting with Grandad's grandfather."

Joanna looked puzzled and asked why there were two sheets.

The answer was really quite simple. There was not enough room to put the names of all the relatives going back in time from both of Grandad's grandparents on one large sheet of paper.

Joanna was clearly showing great interest in everything that Granma had said so far, but by her body language, Thelma could tell she was not totally sure about something and Thelma was pretty sure that she knew what it was.

Joanna's next statement was a fairly obvious one, one that Thelma knew she would make.

"Grandad has got a lot of relatives, hasn't he, Granma?"

"Yes" Thelma said, knowing full well what Joanna would ask next. But then the phone rang. Thelma walked across the room to answer it. It was Mrs Eckersley from across the street asking Thelma if she could collect a prescription from the doctor's for her, sometime in the next few days.

As Thelma stood there with the phone pressed against her ear, she watched Joanna put her finger on Granma's box on the first sheet, run her finger all round it and would have seen no lines going up from it. She leaned over and did the same on the other sheet. Then she turned it upside down to see if there was anything written on the back but there wasn't. She then did the same with the first sheet and again saw no names on that either. Seeing that Granma had now put the phone down, she said: "Granma, where are your mummy and your daddy and all your relatives? I can't see them anywhere. Can you show them to me, please?"

"Let's go and sit down on the big chair and do some talking."

Joanna loved it when Granma said 'do some talking'. She loved sitting there on Granma's lap and listening to all sorts of interesting stories. Granma was so nice to be with and so clever as well. She must surely be one of the cleverest people in the world, Joanna must have often thought. Every time she sat there, she learned something interesting and now she expected to be told all about Granma's relatives. And after that, Granma would start doing the

85

tickling, which was such fun for the little girl. But it would not be like that today because Granma was going to tell Joanna something that would bring tears to both their eyes.

Thelma sat down and lifted Joanna up onto her lap and said:

"When Grandad was growing up in Chisnall Avenue, lots of his relatives lived nearby. When he started doing his family tree, he would ask them about themselves and what they knew about all their relatives from a long time ago. He talked to lots and lots of people that he knew. That is why there are the names of so many of his relatives on these two sheets of paper."

"Didn't he ask any of your relatives as well? Did he forget?"

Such an innocent question from the little one.

"When I was growing up, I lived in a place called Wales. I only came to live here in Ashurst when I was 18 years old."

She looked closely into Joanna's face and it was as though the little girl knew what was coming. But how could she know. She was only five years old.

Thelma swallowed, took a deep breath and went on: "You see Joanna, when I was a baby, my mummy died. That's why I don't know anything about her or any of her relatives."

"And what about your daddy? Didn't he have any relatives?"

"I don't know anything about him either. The war was on then and my daddy was in it. He was in a ship that sailed all over the world. That is why I never met him."

"Didn't he know that your mummy had died and you were all alone in the house? Didn't anybody tell him?"

"I don't think that he knew. His ship was many, many miles away and for months at a time as well."

"That was not very nice for you. If I had been your daddy, I wouldn't have left you all on your own. I would have come home and looked after you."

"I'm sure you would have Joanna and I am sure he would have done that too if he could have, but he was not allowed to. It was war time. It was a bad time for everybody in the country."

They looked closely into each other's eyes and on their cheeks, tears were beginning to fall. It was a big shock to Joanna hearing such a sad tale from her grandmother for the very first time. It was sad for Thelma too. Her childhood days were over 60 years ago now and it was a long time since she had talked to anyone about her past. But now her memories came flooding back.

86

Both held each other tightly. The bond between them had always been strong. Now it was even stronger. They sat there quietly, then after maybe four or five or six minutes or even longer, into the room came Rebecca, Thelma's daughter and Joanna's mother to see two of the most important people in her life, sat there together with tears falling on their cheeks.

"Oh dear. What's wrong? Has something happened to Josh or Neil? Please God no."

Joanna rushed across the room and held her hands out to be picked up and said: "Did you know that when Granma was a baby, her mummy died and she was all alone in the house and her daddy never came to see her. It's so sad and it's making me cry."

"Yes, I did know Joanna, but that was all a long, long time ago. Granma is not alone now, is she? She's got lots of relatives and she's got lots of friends. She's got Grandad, you, Josh, me and your daddy. Uncle Robert and Megan, Phil and Janice next door, Mrs Eckersley across the street, Mr and Mrs Liptrot and Mrs Bottomley. Then there's Joyce and all the girls who work in the shop with her. And then there are all the people that she meets when she goes to watch the Saints. So, don't you worry. Go and give her a big kiss and tell her that you love her and that will make her very happy."

Joanna climbed back on to Granma's lap, kissed her and said: "I'll always look after you, Granma. I'll always be your friend."

"Will you help me whenever I need any help as well?"

"Yes, I will. Promise."

"Can you help me now? At this very moment."

"Yes, Granma."

"This is what I want you to do. Go into the kitchen, switch on the oven and set it at 190 degrees. Then get the turkey out of the fridge. Put it on the baking tray which will probably need a good wash first and pour some cooking oil over it. Oh dear, I think we've run out of oil so you will have to go to ASDA first to get some. Can you also get some washing up liquid as well while you are there and half a dozen large eggs? I'll give you a £10 note. I think that will be enough to pay for it all."

Joanna sat there quite puzzled and looked across to her mother. Granma often asked her to give her some help, but it was always something that they did together in the house or in the garden. It was never to do anything as difficult as going shopping all the way to ASDA and by herself as well.

87

"She's only joking Joanna. You know that when Granma starts joking she's happy and being here with you sat on her lap is making her very happy."

Joanna looked back at Granma, but still thinking that what she had asked her to do, was still what she had to do, said quietly: "Granma, will you come to ASDA with me, please?"

"I was only joking. I finished all the shopping yesterday."

Then she picked up a couple of tissues and said: "I'll wipe your tears away and you can wipe mine away."

As they were doing that, in walked her daddy and her brother Josh. He had been with his cousins at their house at Collins Green and now had a plaster on his leg, the result of an accident, riding John's new bicycle in their garden.

Soon after, her parents decided that it was time to go home. Thelma wagged her finger at Neil and said: "No drinking and driving tonight, you two. Get yourselves a taxi. It's not that far to Penketh from your house, is it?"

"It's all right Mum. We are not going to Joan's now. She has gone down with the flu so we are all meeting for a drink in The Chapel and we can all walk back to our house from there instead."

After they had left, Thelma asked the grandchildren what they wanted to do next. Joanna wanted to carry on with the jigsaw in the front room. Josh wanted to carry on reading the Arthur Mee encyclopaedias that were also kept in there. They were the very same ones that Thelma herself had loved to read when, as an 18 year old, she had first lived in the house with Alan's grandparents during that terrible winter of 1962 to 1963.

So off the children went into the front room. Alan brought out two bottles of beer from the pantry and told Thelma that while he had been out in town, he had seen Big Joan in Bridge Street. She had once been in charge of the Print Room when Thelma had first started work at Wilkinson's in 1962 and had always been a very good friend to them both.

After they had finished their tea, Thelma asked the children what they wanted to do next. There were lots of games that they could all play. There was Ludo, Chinese Checkers, I Spy and Animals. But by now Joanna had told Josh about what had happened earlier in the day and both of them now wanted to know more about all relatives in the family from a long time ago.

With the two sheets back on the table, Alan took over and had

88

something to say about almost everybody whose name was written on them. In every box was written their name, date of birth, marriage and death. Alan also knew what work most of his relatives had done during their lives. Going back to 1799, collier, woodworker, bottle hand and labourer were the main occupations of most of the men on his grandfather's side of the family. He was born in 1889 in Fingerpost in St Helens but around the time that 'Ned' was due to leave school his family had flitted to Ashurst, just a few miles away.

On his grandmother's side, things were slightly different because sometime in the 1860s, her mother's parents had come to live in Ashurst from somewhere in North Wales, though nobody knew quite why and exactly where from. Then at the age of 18, her mother, Elizabeth Pickavance had married John Tabern, a face worker at the Southport Edge Colliery and one of four brothers who lived in Fenton Street with their widowed mother.

They spent over an hour on the family tree, but by this time Thelma could see that Josh had lost interest and Joanna had had enough for one day. She took the sheets back upstairs and when she came back, she saw that Joanna was sat on Grandad's knee and Josh was back into the front room. As she was making a drink for them all in the kitchen, she heard Joanna ask: "Grandad, did you have to go to Wales to find Granma? Was she waiting for you?"

So Alan explained that he had got to know Granma when she first started work at Wilkinson's and then went on to tell her how he had met Granma on Christmas Eve and taken her to Mario's coffee bar. It was there that he had discovered that she was going to be on her own all over Christmas.

"Did you know that she had no Mummy and no Daddy?"

"That was when she told me, so I invited her to spend Christmas Day here with all our family and after that, Granma began to live here with my Granny and Grandad."

"You were very kind, Grandad. Was Granma pleased?"

"Yes, she was. She loved living here with them then and she loves living here with me now and she loves people coming to see her as well. And lots of people do come to see her."

"Did your Granny like Granma?"

"Yes, she loved her."

"Was your Granny nice?"

It was one of Joanna's favourite questions about people and it brought a lump to Alan's throat as he replied: "Yes, she was very

89

nice and so was my Grandad as well."

"Have you got any pictures of them?"

"Yes. Do you want to see them?"

"Yes please."

"I'll go and get the box out while you go and have a wash. We don't want your grubby little fingers spoiling them, do we? Some of these photographs are very, very old."

Soon the table was covered with photographs of around 50 of Grandad's' relatives, some going back nearly 80 years. But there were only four of Granma's photograph's to look at.

After over an hour had been spent looking at them, Joanna picked out her three favourites. One was Alan's mother stood with Alan and his brother Paul and sister Joan in the back garden of their home in Chisnall Avenue. One was of Alan's Granny with a lovely big smile on her face making a cake in the kitchen but Joanna's favourite photograph was one of Thelma's mother and father stood outside a large building in this place called Wales.

Grandad carefully put all the photographs into the box and took it back upstairs. Joanna went and sat on Granma's lap and asked her what her daddy's name was: "When I tell you his name, I know what you will say."

"What?"

"You'll say that's a funny name."

"Why, what is it?"

"Yiorgos Angelopoulos."

"That's a funny name."

"Well he came from Greece. And he grew up in a town that has also got a funny name."

"What is it?"

"Thrakomakedhones."

"That's another funny name."

"What was he like, Granma? Was he nice?"

"I don't know, Joanna. I never met him. The war was on and he was away all the time on a big ship."

Joanna looked up into her grandmother's eyes and quietly said:

"I'm going to be very brave this time, Granma. I'm not going to cry again."

And with that, the little girl burst into tears: "Don't cry, little one. I'm not alone now, am I. Look at all the relatives and friends that I've got. And there's Little Ted as well."

90

"Who's Little Ted?"

"He lives upstairs."

"Really! Who is he?"

"When I was a little girl growing up, Little Ted was my best friend. Have you not met him yet? Let's go and see what he is doing. He is probably fast asleep but he'll really love to meet you."

And with that, the two of them went upstairs to the back bedroom, with Joanna holding Granma's hand very tightly. It almost seemed as though she was frightened. Thelma opened the top drawer to reveal him lay there, under a blanket.

"Hallo Little Ted. Have we woken you up? I've brought Joanna to see you. She's one of our family."

Then she picked up the much loved, battered old doll that she had had for most of her life, gave him to Joanna to hold and said:

"Stay there and tell him about where you live and what you like to do at school. I'm going to get my camera out because I want to take a photo of the two of you stood there together."

Later and with more than a dozen photos of Little Ted and Joanna taken, Thelma said: "When you are fast asleep in bed tonight. I am going to press a few buttons on my computer and do some magic and tomorrow when you get back home, these photographs will be inside your mummy's computer. What do you think about all of that?"

Joanna could not quite take it all in. Well, it had been a very busy day for her. It had also been quite a sad day too and parts of it had been very sad. But, in a very moving way, the little girl, who later was to become one of the leading members of the Great English Bus Pass Revolution of 2025 was introduced to the wonderful world of the internet.

14. New Year's Day 2008

Joanna's parents arrived the following morning in a taxi. This was because they had drunk too much the previous night and were both probably still over the limit. Rebecca went into the kitchen to tell her mother what had happened at the party. Then she asked her where the children were, assuming that they must both be still fast asleep upstairs. But her mother's reply totally shocked her.

"I'm not exactly sure where they are, Rebecca. Last night I asked them to carry out an old Welsh tradition for me. They had to go out of the house by the back door just before midnight, walk all round the house and come back in through the front door just after midnight and bring the New Year in with them."

"And!"

"Well they haven't come back yet so I thought they must have decided to go home. I thought that you would be bringing them with you today in your car."

Before Rebecca could have a heart attack, they heard footsteps on the stairs and in to the kitchen rushed Joanna carrying something wrapped in a blanket.

"Mummy. This is Little Ted. He lives upstairs and he's my new friend."

"Mother! I almost had a heart attack then."

"Do you honestly think I would have done anything like that?"

Then turning to Joanna, Thelma said: "Haven't you got a silly mummy. Does she really think that I would let you two out of my sight for even one little minute?"

Later, with the children playing in the front room and with Rebecca and Thelma in the kitchen, Neil asked his father in law what his predictions for the New Year were.

"The Saints will have another good season, Tony Blair will continue to make a lot of money talking about how to solve all the world's problems that he and George Bush have caused in the first place and you will continue to stay in the Labour Party, while disagreeing with most of the things that it has ever done."

"Alan, you will be pleased to hear that the four of us jacked our membership in about a month ago. I have just never had the chance to get round to telling you."

"What was it that finally made the four of you decide to do that?"

"It's an interesting tale."

"Go on then, tell me. I'm always interested to hear how some folk managed to be members of an organisation that I left over 40 years ago and have never felt the need to go back to since."

So then Neil explained what he and his three buddies had been considering doing for quite some time: "I thought that New Labour did a lot of good things at first. There was the Northern Ireland Peace Agreement, more cash put into the NHS, the National Minimum Wage although they set it far too low, free TV licences for the over-75s, free off-peak local bus travel for the over 60s, set up over 2,000 Sure Start Centres and brought in the Working Family Tax Credits to support low paid parents in work and help pay for their child care.

But all that was ruined by the invasion of Iraq in 2003. Despite that, we all stayed in it because it meant that we could still play snooker in the Labour Club and drink the ale which was top dog and cheap too.

Then a few weeks ago Len's daughter Ann came home from college and he invited us round to meet her and listen to her tell us what she thought about the Labour Government.

She started off by saying that everything Labour had done was based around free market, pro-business politics and driven by the idea that 'The market knows best' which was just a euphemism for giving corporate business greater control of the economy.

They had turned a blind eye to all the tax dodging by the multinationals and had failed to renationalise the railways preferring to hand out vast tax payer funded subsidies to keep the whole shambolic mess going.

They had refused to even try to regulate the privatised utilities companies which were now creaming off high profits out of the general public and had kick started the privatisation of the NHS.

They had failed to invest in much needed social housing, had overseen the privatisation of much council housing stock into the hands of privately operated undemocratic housing associations and had kept Britain with some of the most restrictive trade union laws in Europe.

She then explained what PFI was. It was an arrangement under which the private sector was heavily involved in the funding, designing, building and financing of so called public sector projects, then leasing them to the government in contracts that might last

93

up to 50 years. And at the end of that 50 years they would then revert back to being owned by these original private sector companies.

She talked for over an hour and summed it all up at the end by describing the 'New Labour' administration as little more than a Murdoch backed, neo-liberal alternative Tory Party enthusiastically following Thatcherite policies.

Listening to her talk was a real eye-opener for us. She must know more about politics and economics than the four of us put together, and she's not even 21 yet! And yet to be honest, everything that she said all seemed to make sense.

The following week I bumped into one of my dad's old pals in Warrington. Harry had been a Labour man since the year dot but no longer. He said that he hadn't left the Labour Party though, but that the Labour Party had left him, which was quite a good way of describing what a lot of party members round here now think."

"So what was it that finally made you all decide to leave?"

"It was the proposal to close Shell Lane Surgery and replace it with one to be built on Bolton Road financed by a PFI deal. I wanted to discuss it at our monthly members' meeting but Cyril was chairman said we couldn't because in his view the agenda was full and in his view, PFIs were a great idea anyway.

Mrs Hall asked why couldn't we leave any discussion on the party having a float on next year's Ashurst Carnival until the next meeting and discuss this new surgery instead.

Len then said that as far as he was concerned, PFI could be summed up as 'get one new hospital built but pay for two' and if Gordon Brown thought it was public money well spent, then he was either working for the banks or he was a fool.

Cyril said that if he thought that about the Prime Minister there was no place for him in the Labour Party and he would do us all a favour if he closed the door on his way out. Len looked at me, nodded towards it and the four of us got up and walked out and much to our surprise Mr and Mrs Hall came out with us too.

As we were all stood outside, deciding what to do next, Cyril appeared. I thought he was going to ask us all to come back in, but it wasn't anything like that. He said that we would all still have to pay our subs until the end of the month to which Andy replied: 'We'll see you in court first, pal.'

We all went up to the Sefton, to decide what we were going to

94

do next. As usual we talked with Jack in there. He told us that the brewery were moving him to The Wigan Arms next month. Then he went on to say that he would be very pleased to see us all up there and how he would continue to enjoy listening to us endlessly discussing how we were going to reorganise the world."

"So what are the four of you all going to do now?"

"I am going to do what Ken is going to do which is read some of the many books I've had for years and in some cases never had the time to even open. Ken broke his leg last week playing football and so reading will be a good way for him to spend his time."

"How will you ever find the time to do any reading?"

"They are operating on my knee next week and no doubt after that I'll be told to rest it and as it was the firm's fault that the accident happened in the first place, I'll still be on full pay."

"What about Andy and Len?"

"Andy got made redundant again a month ago. He went up to Aberdeen to see his mother and while he was up there, he got offered a job at a firm that he once worked at. Luckily for him, his brother Hamish has gone back to work in Norway so he and Ann are going to live in his house for a while."

"How will Ann like living up in Aberdeen? She never really settled in Ashurst, did she?"

"No."

"Where did she live before she came to live here?"

"The top of Billinge!"

"I bet you'll miss having him around, won't you."

"We will. Top man was Andy."

"So what are you going to read first?"

"What would you suggest?"

"*The Ragged Trousered Philanthropist.* It was written by a Liverpool painter and decorator called Robert Tressell. He based it on the time he spent working on the South Coast. I can still remember one particular quote from it: Every man who is not helping to bring about a better state of affairs for the future is helping to perpetuate the present misery and is therefore the enemy of his own children. There is no such thing as being neutral: we must either help or hinder."

"And what are you reading at the moment?"

"*Rugby League in Twentieth Century Britain.* It's all about how our game has always been closely linked with its local community."

95

"And what's Thelma reading?"

"*Bloody Foreigners. The story of immigration to Britain.*" I read the first page but there's one big problem with it for me."

"What's that?"

"It's all in Welsh."

"You're joking."

"Well you should know me by now."

"I do."

"I said to her the only reason she was reading it, was because she's an immigrant herself. Do you know what she said to that?"

"'After you have read the first few chapters, you will soon realise that we are all the children of immigrants. It just depends how far back you go and of course, as usual, she's right."

Before any more could be said, Robert and Megan arrived and a few minutes later they were all sat round the table having their lunch and with Rebecca saying first: "Mum says that you are thinking of finishing work soon, dad."

"We all might be, but I've just about had enough of it, now Rebecca. I've worked there for over 50 years and been all over Europe installing what I've designed and drawn. Now, all that our boss, Duffy, is interested in, is if any changes had to be made on site and if they had, why and who would have to pay for it."

"So how many countries have you been to?"

"If I include all the holidays that I have had abroad as well, I reckon that except for Iceland, Cyprus, Finland and Luxembourg I must have been to every country in Western Europe. I've also been to Poland, Hungary, the old Yugoslavia, Greece and Tunisia."

"Which was the best one?"

"I can't tell you that while your mother is in the room."

"Dad!"

"Have you never been to America, Alan?" asked Neil.

"No, but I remember now that I did once go to Argentina. One Thursday I had wired up a machine that was going to a trade exhibition over there. The plan was for it to go down to the docks on the Saturday morning, but on the Friday, one of the electronic boards was removed for some reason and it never got put back.

"When the machine got switched on in the exhibition hall, it would only run in slow speed. So I had to take the missing board out there and connect it up, which took me about an hour. The guy in charge asked me to stay on, just in case anything else went

96

wrong and so I had to spend the rest of the week lying on the beach which was little more than 10 minutes walk away."

Alan had always enjoyed being at work, but now he had reached the age when he would prefer to spend his time doing something totally different. One thing was to sort out his large collection of football and rugby programmes and at the same time find some photographs he was sure he had put somewhere 'safe'.

One was him and Charlie Eccleston talking to Harold Wilson in Thatto Heath Labour Club just before the 1964 General Election. Another was him outside the American Embassy in 1968, on a huge demonstration against the Vietnam War, and a third was with his pal Eric Yates and Eric's Uncle Len, a train driver, stood on the foot plate of his Patriot class locomotive number 45534 and named *E Total Broadhurst* in Shaw Street Station in St Helens.

Later that evening Thelma thought about how Rebecca had told Joanna about all the people that Granma now knew. Some were the people she had known at Wilkinson's. Others were the girls that she worked with in the Oxfam shop and some of their customers. Others were neighbours and all the people who she had become friendly with, while watching the Saints.

There was Brenda from Haresfinch, Maureen from Doulton Street and Joan from the top of Moss Bank. Thelma had first become friendly with her partly because of something they both had in common. It was the fact that both their faces were covered with freckles, not that it bothered either of them now, although it might have done when they were still at their junior schools.

Another person she knew well was their good friend Joyce. After her husband Sam had died, she had kept in touch with them for a while but now they rarely saw her. A good enough reason to visit her the next day, Thelma decided.

As soon as they walked into her house though, it was clear that Joyce was not well. The place was very untidy, quite surprising since Joyce had always been the most tidy of people. When Thelma asked her if she was ill, all that Joyce could say was that she would be all right when Sam came home from work!

"Would you like us to give the place a good clean?"

Joyce had nodded in a very disinterested way.

"We'll come on Thursday if that's all right."

"I think that she has lost the will to live" said Alan later, as they drove home.

"I think you're right, Alan. In fact I don't think there is much we can do for her, but the least we can do is tidy the place up a bit. That kitchen is beginning to smell."

On Thursday when they knocked on the front door there was no answer. They went round the side and opened the back door. They went upstairs and found their friend, no longer of this world. Maybe she was now with the great love of her life, Sam Holroyd, the good Yorkshireman from Mytholmroyd.

What a terrible shock it was for them both. Joyce had always been such a good friend, as had Sam. But then, going back in time so had Charlie, Mick, Len, Stan, Dickie, Paul, Les, Big Joan, Rita, Hazel and many others, whose names flashed through Alan's head as they drove home. Where were they all now? Maybe they were all together, looking down on him from up in the sky and pleased to see that he was still with that young Welsh girl, the one with all the freckles and always so shabbily dressed.

"What are you thinking, Alan? You are pretty quiet for once."

"Whenever someone I know dies, it often leaves me thinking about whatever happens next."

"Well, one thing is for sure if there is something else, you can be sure that she will have just met Sam and will be talking to him 10 to the dozen right now."

"Yes, but what state will he be in, virtually paralysed and maybe brain dead as well, like he was the very last time we saw him. Would he even recognise her?"

"I don't know Alan. I just don't know."

A few days later Alan received a phone call from Duffy, who had a very simple question for him. Would he like to work in America for a year? Amsterdam had linked up with a company based in Baltimore that had a lot of work for him to do and the pay would be very good.

Alan's first reaction was to decline the offer. It might be an experience, living on the other side of the Atlantic, but not necessarily a good one. Perhaps he could take Thelma with him, at least for some of the time but then he would miss watching the Saints, bowling in Victoria Park, meeting old workmates and helping his grandchildren grow up.

As he sat there the following evening, mulling over what Duffy had said, Rebecca and Joanna came into the room. Rebecca went into the kitchen to see her Mum and as Joanna sat on his knee, he

98

told her that he had something very important to ask her.

"What is it, Grandad?"

"What would you think if I went to work in America for a year and Granma came with me?"

"I would be sad because I would miss seeing you both a lot."

"What would you think if I went there on my own and Granma stayed here?"

"That would make Granma very sad because she would be all alone and she would miss you and I would miss you too."

"You would still come and visit here, wouldn't you?"

"Yes. I'll come every day if Granma wants me to."

"Finally one more question for you. What would you think if we took you to Southport in the car one day next week?"

"Yes please. Can Josh come?"

"Of course he can come as long as he doesn't turn up wearing his flipping rugby boots."

Alan smiled to himself. He had answered his own question. There was no way he was going to spend a year in America and not see Joanna, Josh and Daisy growing up and not being able to watch the Saints playing the greatest game almost every week.

"Let's go and see what day Granma can come with us."

"Granma, what would you think if I told you that Joanna doesn't want me and you to go to America and wants us to take her and Josh to Southport next week in the car instead?"

"If that is what Joanna wants, well that's good enough for me."

Then she said something that seemed quite ridiculous, but could well be construed by some people as being very true: "Anyway, I think that Southport is much better than America. I bet they don't have any streets as nice as Lord Street over there."

With that, Alan knew that he had just turned down his last chance to visit America, not that he had ever really wanted to go there. However he still had hopes of revisiting the areas near to some of the chemical plants, cotton mills and power stations that he had once spent time at in Europe and particularly those at Familicao, west of Porto, Gyor in Western Hungary and the steel works at Duisburg in West Germany.

The following day they had a phone call from Alan's brother. On retiring from work, Paul and his wife Dorothy had bought a house near to the town of Calasparra in Murcia in Spain. Alan and Thelma had visited them three times and each time Dorothy had encouraged them to do what they had done. But Thelma's reaction each time was to say 'no'. There was no way that she was going to miss helping Josh, Joanna and Daisy, grow up.

There was no way that she would ever want to leave the house, which held so many happy memories for her, going right back to the winter of 1962 and 1963. It was also a place from where she could so easily walk up to Windle Steps cemetery and 'reconnect' with an old Lancashire lady who had done so much for her when, as a teenager, she had needed a lot of loving care and attention.

Alan also was not keen to go and live abroad either. He had always enjoyed visiting Calasparra, but all he wanted to do now was to stay in Ashurst with the rest of his family, meet old friends, watch the Saints and help Southport Edge Miners' Welfare get promoted into Ashurst Crown Green League Division One.

However he did feel guilty about not going up to the east coast of Scotland more often to see his sister Joan. This was where she now lived following the sad death of her husband Ray in 1978.

After his funeral service at Christ Church in Eccleston, she had accepted an invitation from his sister Pamela to visit her. She stayed for a week the first time, stayed for a fortnight the second time and then on returning home, had decided to sell her house in Rainford and go and live close to the sea front at Stonehaven.

Now she was fully enjoying a new lifestyle along with a lot of new friends, many of them members of the Green Party of which she had become a keen and active member.

She had also taken up painting, gardening and much to Alan's surprise and amazement, she had also started playing snooker again. This was something that she had been quite good at when she was in her early twenties and when she was spending most of her spare time in the Trades Club. And a couple of years earlier at the grand old age of 67 and watched by just about everybody in the place, she had once made a break of just 67!

15. The day Harold Wilson was in Paris

Before the trip to Southport could be arranged, Joanna went down with a bad cold and so it was two weeks later before she was well enough to go out for the day. Soon after Rebecca had brought her round, they set off.

Alan drove through the New Bold Estate, under the bridge at St Helens Junction and stopped outside a house in Herbert Street, where he spent a few minutes with an old friend, who had just come out of hospital. Then he drove along Robins Lane, past the site of the old UGB factory, soon to be the location for the Saints new ground, through the town centre, up Greenfield Road and on to Windle Island, crossed the East Lancs Road and shortly after turned right into Rainford and stopped again. He went into a house close to the Derby Arms and reappeared a few minutes later carrying a large cardboard box.

In it was a collection of rugby league programmes that once belonged to an old pal who had recently passed away. Then it was back onto the Rainford Bypass and on towards Southport. As they approached Ormskirk, they passed the garden centre that his old school friend Winston once owned. No longer though, Winston was now living in America in Florida.

Four hours later they were all back in Burtonwood and as soon as they had finished their evening meal, Joanna asked if she could go to bed. The sea air had clearly knocked her out. Soon after, Rebecca told Thelma that Joanna had not really been herself for the last couple of weeks. It was not just her being ill and in bed for much of the time with a very bad cough. It was also because of what Granma had told her about when she was a little baby.

"Do you know what she said to me last week, Mum? She said when Granma was a little girl and had no mummy and no daddy, did she have to make all her own meals and go to ASDA by herself to do the shopping?"

"She's a little love, isn't she? So what did you tell her about my early life?"

"I told her that you lived in a big house with lots of other children who didn't have a mummy or a daddy and you all had a lovely time. Did I say the right thing?"

"Well, there were some good things about that place in Cardiff, but not a lot but it doesn't matter now. What's important is that Joanna does not get too upset about it all. Maybe we should take her out in the car a bit more, but I'll do whatever you think will be best for her. And with Josh as well whenever he can spare some time from playing rugby."

"Or looking after Noah" laughed his mum.

Noah was the latest addition to the Rigby household. It was a small kitten that had been a Christmas present for the whole family from their auntie Jenny and uncle Dave who lived at Penwortham near Preston. It was something that Joanna liked a little bit but which Josh had become almost obsessed with.

A couple of days later, Rebecca brought Joanna into the house. She was taking Josh to the doctor's and didn't want to take Joanna there as well. But as soon as she had gone, Thelma remembered that she had promised to collect a prescription for Mrs Eckersley. Alan had the car and it was too far to take Joanna to the Health Centre, the chemist's and do some shopping in ASDA as well. The best thing was to see if her next door neighbour could look after Joanna for a couple of hours.

No problem there. Janice was always more than happy to help. She was going nowhere, so there was no need for Thelma to rush. And so it was a couple of hours later, before she returned. She went next door to collect Joanna and was greeted with something she was very pleased to hear from her neighbour.

"You've just come back at the right time. I've made some rag pudding for us dinner so you can both have some if you want to."

"Is that some special oriental delicacy from Oldham?"

"No" said Janice with a big smile on her face. "It's from Bury."

A couple of days later, Thelma bumped into Janice in the Post Office, walked back home with her and was then invited in. She always enjoyed talking to Janice and was also interested to know how she and Joanna had got on together. Her neighbour's answer was very interesting: "The first thing I did was to make her a drink of orange juice. Then I asked her where did she live, how old she was, and what she liked to do at school. Then I told her that she had a very nice pair of grandparents and how I enjoyed living next door to you both. And then do you know what she said to me?"

"Did you know that when Granma was a little girl, she had no mummy and no daddy and she lived in a big house with lots of other children. That's not right, is it?"

"Yes, it is. You see my mother died when I was a baby. It was 1944, the war was on and my father was away at sea and so I was brought up in a home in Cardiff. Joanna only found all this out a few weeks ago and it has really upset her."

"Oh, I am sorry."

"Well it's hardly a problem now. It was over 60 years ago. Do you want to know more? I bet you do."

"I'd love to but only if you want to tell me. Not if it is in any way painful for you to recall."

"It's not now and it's interesting. But how long have you got?"

"Phil will be back around tea time, so I'd say about five hours."

"That's cutting it a bit fine."

"Do you think it might help if we opened a bottle of wine?"

And so Thelma proceeded to tell Janice about her early life in Cardiff, working at the holiday camp in Rhyl, then in a hotel in Liverpool and coming to Ashurst when she was 18 years old. Then she told her about how she had first met Alan at work and what had happened on that fateful Christmas Eve in 1962.

Then she asked if Janice had a tale to tell about her past.

"I have but not today. Have you seen the time? But just come in the front room for a minute and have a look at some paintings I've done recently."

The first one was based on a painting by Camille Pissaro showing Napoleon sitting on a horse, but with the reins being held by Mrs Eckersley! Another was one of her partner Phil dressed in a Saints kit sitting on the shoulders of Keiron Cunningham and Paul Wellens and her latest was the reproduction of a copy of *Louvecienne* which had also been painted by Pissaro. Or rather it was two-thirds of the original painting, a couple walking along a road in the middle of a French village. But behind them, Janice had painted an Oldham Corporation bus, being driven by Phil!

That evening, they decided to go for a drink in the *Ring o' Bells*. Within five minutes of sitting down in the best room, they were joined by their neighbours Margery and Cyril.

"We've just been to your mansion to see if you wanted to come out for a drink with us and here you are, sat here, the pair of you" was Cyril's opening comment.

"We are only staying here for a couple of hours and then we are off clubbing down Liverpool, so I hope you have got something interesting to tell us."

103

"If I mentioned the name John Rigby would that qualify as being something that might be interesting to tell you?"

"If it is about John Rigby, it is bound to be interesting. Just let me turn my hearing aid up."

Cyril then proceeded to tell them that he had met 'Riggers' in Waterstones in Manchester the previous week and had had a few beers with him in the *Moon under Water* on Deansgate.

"You know that him and his band went to Amsterdam after he left your place back in the 1970s. Well, they did fairly well for a couple of years until their drummer Steve had to come back to Prescot to get married. Then, Phil had grown so fond of some magic pills that he started to go round the bend and all this led to the band breaking up. John stayed there and went back to working on the drawing board and spending much of his time and wealth discussing the meaning of life with half naked women like you can do quite easily in Amsterdam.

Sometime later he was in a night club when a fire broke out. As everybody was rushing out of the place he heard a woman up above screaming and so he went up the stairs and rescued her and her baby. Sadly, the baby died from the smoke while John and her suffered minor burns and soon after they started living together. Now, this woman's uncle was a local property developer and soon after, he employed John on various enterprises that he was involved in. However John soon discovered that they were involved in the sale of drugs and protection rackets.

Then he started getting leaned on by some criminal elements. So he decided it would be safer for him to leave Amsterdam and is now living at Shaw in Oldham, although he didn't say exactly why there or who with.

He asked how you were and whether you were still married to Thelma. I've got his telephone number and I've given him mine, as well but he said he wouldn't ring me for a bit as he had stuff in London to deal with. I haven't a clue what that means, but knowing him there's bound to be something unusual or unbelievable about it, as you might well imagine."

"I certainly do, probably something as good or as daft as the time he upset Harold Wilson's election campaign in 1964 although that might have been before you started at the BI?"

"I might have heard this one before but go on tell us."

"John was in the Young Socialists then and early one morning about a week before the election, a moulder from the Iron Foundry told him that their local MP, Harold Wilson, was doing a factory gate lunch time meeting outside Rye Hey gates. So John tells all his mates in the drawing office to pass the word on. Not surprisingly it went all round the factory. That would have been when around 17,000 people worked there.

"This bloke told John that Wilson would be there just before half twelve. So a lot of people who normally had their dinner in the main canteen on Warrington Road, decided to get something to eat at that little pie shop instead. By half twelve there must have been around 500 people stood around on the pavement but no Harold Wilson. Soon after there was twice that number there plus reporters from the *Prescot Reporter* and the *Liverpool Echo* and then a police car but still no Mr Wilson. By five to one everybody started drifting back to work, including a lot of hungry people who had just found that the little pie shop had run out of all its pies!

"That night on the *BBC News*, Harold Wilson was interviewed just after he had landed at Gatwick Airport, having spent the day talking to the French President in Paris. I remember seeing that interview and clearly the last thing on Wilson's mind at the time, was about a thousand members of his constituency going without their dinner waiting for him to talk to them in their dinner hour.

"The next day John had a right go at this moulder. Of course everybody who worked in the Iron Foundry or who worked in the whole of the Accessories Division knew that Tommy Litherland was just one big wind up merchant and so they all laughed their socks off at Mr Hopeless from Hope Street!

"I don't think that John ever lived that down. It's probably the main reason why he left the BI, I reckon."

16. 'The Dream'

It was now February and Neil was back home after the operation on his knee and Alan and Thelma had called round to see how he was. Five minutes after they arrived, there was a knock on the door. It was John Sutton, an old friend of Neil's. For the last 15 years he had been living in Coventry, but following the death of his mother, he and his wife had decided to return to Ashurst to live in her old house. Once they had settled in, the first thing John did, was to visit his old pal. It was a pure coincidence that it was so soon after Neil had returned home from St Helens Hospital.

The two of them had been pals for years. As a teenager, Neil had been in the Young Socialists whereas John had never shown much interest in politics. As they grew older, Neil had joined the Labour Party while John had just continued to be an active member of the Amalgamated Engineering Union. Then on being made redundant at Hilton's Assembly, and no work around, John had moved to Coventry to work at Rolls Royce.

They quickly realised that John's views about Britain today were quite similar to their own, particularly when he had talked about how Attlee's Labour Government had still created the NHS, a social housing programme and almost full employment for all, at a time when the country was virtually bankrupt. With its reduced emphasis on them now though, New Labour was losing the support of many of its traditional supporters, something that Alan was keenly looking forward to discussing with Jennifer at lunchtime the following day.

However, she was not there when he arrived, because later that morning she was going to a funeral in Wigan. But it wouldn't have mattered if she had been there, because as soon as he walked into his office, Duffy asked him to go to Eggborough Power Station and two hours later he was signing in at their gate house.

By three o'clock, he was ready to leave when Richard, an engineer and an old friend of his, appeared. Knowing what he was like, Alan feared he might now have to spend another hour with him and particularly so when Richard said that he had an important question that he wanted answering. Fortunately it had nothing to do with the generation of high voltage electrical power.

"Alan, you know that the Northern Union started at that meeting in the George Hotel in 1895 and the first season they still played to all the old rules and 15-a-side. My question for you is this. When did they reduce the number of players to 13?"

One of Alan's great interests in life was the history of rugby league and so he was more than pleased to answer the question for his Yorkshire pal: "It was first discussed at the 1906 AGM of the Northern Union. Warrington wanted to reduce the number of players to 13. They said their proposal would make the game faster, easier to form the scrum and would save every club about £100 every year. Leigh agreed with them and so did Whitehaven and Wath Brow. St Helens though, only wanted it reduced to 14 players.

The Wakefield delegate said that he did not know of a single instance where teams in any of the town's workshop competitions ever had more than 12 players. After some discussion it was put to the vote and it was carried by 43 votes to 18."

"Why were Whitehaven and Wath Brow there? Whitehaven only joined after the war and Wath Brow never have done."

"Any club that was affiliated to the Northern Union could attend and vote and so at that meeting were probably all the professional clubs along with many of the top amateur clubs."

"Thanks for that. It means that I have just won 10 quid off my brother. He thought they changed to 13 players at the start of the third season. I was sure he was wrong. So I told him that I would ask the Lord and if he didn't know then I'd ask one of his Saints."

The following lunchtime, Jennifer told him that she was writing an article about the privatisation of the country's power industry, one which had seen the Central Electricity Generating Board split up into National Power, Power Gen and National Grid in the late 1980s. Then he told her about how much she would have agreed with most of what John had said a couple of nights earlier.

"Do you know what, Alan? Most of these politicians are nothing more than agents for big business. They have little respect for the people they are supposed to represent. Take the issue of poverty. The answer is simple. The causes of poverty are low wages, high rent, poor state benefits for the unemployed, the sick and the vulnerable coupled with ever increasing food and energy prices.

Do you know that behind every poor kid, there is at least one poor adult. Behind every 100,000 poor kids there is at least one excessively rich adult and many children who live in poverty have at least one parent working.

None of them ever declare war on tax havens. It is easier to

107

declare war on the poor, the disabled, the unemployed and the vulnerable and as for Westminster, it's little more than a home of puerile behaviour, archaic practices and endemic corruption."

"Jennifer, whatever has brought about this barnstorming response to what is going on in the world today? Where is the cool and calm lady that we all have come to love and cherish?"

"I was moved by the situation involving a family in Wigan being made homeless that I heard about at that funeral I went to yesterday. I find that I get very emotional when I hear about ordinary decent people who are having to use food banks and are up to their eyes in debt, through absolutely no fault of their own."

At that moment Duffy walked in and little more was said about something that had clearly upset their workmate.

Just as they were about to switch *Channel 4 News* on, Ray Hewitt appeared. He had recently returned from visiting his son in Toronto and the first thing they talked about was his black eye. On his last day in Canada, he had been involved in a heated discussion and then a brawl with a loud mouth Texan. All that Ray wanted to say about it now was that, soon afterwards, he had boarded his plane and flown home, whereas the other guy had probably gone to the nearest hospital and by now would have to pay a small fortune to have his broken nose treated.

What was much more interesting for Ray to talk about though was the man who he had sat next to on his journey home. It was a lobbyist for an American insurance company whose long term aim was to gain a foothold in the NHS. With him Ray had pretended to dislike the way he had been treated over the years. The more Ray 'complained' about the NHS, the more Elmer had swallowed it and as the plane was close to landing, he had arranged to send Ray details of how he could make a fortune by investing his capital into various financial ventures.

As Ray took another swig from his drink, Alan asked him now that he was back home what was he going to spend his time "looking into things" next.

"Talking to that prat Elmer has convinced me that I need to find out a lot more about what's happening to the NHS and particularly what the Labour Government have been doing with it since 1997. I have spent the last few days reading something called *Britain's Biggest Enterprise. Ideas for radical reform of the NHS*. It's an article written in 1988 by two MPs, Oliver Letwin and John Redwood and describes in detail their plans for radically reforming the NHS."

"Isn't Letwin the one who wants to privatise the world.?"

"Yes. That's him. After that, I read the *Griffiths Report* which is a document Thatcher commissioned in 1983. Without any real supporting evidence it calls for major changes to the NHS and in effect help start the NHS going down the path of seeing itself more as a business than as a service, suggesting, for example, that GPs get more involved in budgets and commissioning services.

Before I read them though, I already knew that one result of the Tory National Health Service Care Act in 1990 was that all the NHS hospitals had been turned into Trusts. This meant that they had all become self-governing bodies run by boards full of non-executive directors and which no longer reported to their Regional or District Authorities but directly to the Secretary of State.

Each Trust now had to compete with all the other Trusts for 'business' which is their fancy word for providing health care for the public. They all have more freedom to borrow money, generate income and raise revenue directly from providing their services. In fact it now seems that the primary function of a hospital is to make a profit for its shareholders rather than provide good quality health care for the public which is what they were initially set up to do. Also hospitals being now independent will make them much easier to be taken over by any American health care organisations which is essentially what these two MPs would love to see happen."

He took another drink from his glass and continued: "I've also spent some time reading up about the NHS internal market. The bureaucracy of this thing is going to cripple the NHS. There will have to be hours spent checking the paperwork associated with the tendering processes with every individual transaction now requiring a separate invoice. The 1997 Labour Manifesto said that in 1996 this extra cost had been estimated at around £1.5 billion a year. Ten years later, how much more is wasted on it now, I ask myself.

That Manifesto also promised to end the internal market system and individual GP fund holding. It did do but then came their Health and Social Care Act and then Practice Based Commissioning in 2005. At the same time they were also using more PFI schemes to finance the building of new hospitals, something which I reckon will bleed the NHS dry over the next 20 odd years if it hasn't drowned in the bureaucracy by then.

Sorry, for going on a bit but that's just a brief summary of what

109

I have found out so far. I can't be dead sure that everything I have just told you is 100 percent accurate. It's all very complicated, and reading through all these papers and articles is doing my head in. But I think it's good enough for Jennifer to check it all out and see what she and her sister make of it all."

He took another drink from his glass and continued: "A lot of this stuff was going on when Alan Milburn was the Minister of Health, from October 1999 to June 2003, I think it was. What interests me about him is that he was a member of our old union DATA. So I'm going to ring an old mate from Sunderland up to see what he can tell me about the man.

I know he scrapped the Community Health Councils. These were patient based organisations that had been set up in 1974 and funded independently through the Regional Health Authorities with a brief to represent both patients and the public in general.

I knew all about these CHCs because my neighbour was involved in one then and how angry he was when they were abolished. He told me it would stop the public having any say in all the changes that the government were introducing. It must have affected him pretty badly too because a week later, after telling me what he thought about the whole business, he dropped dead in ASDA and he was only 57.

I also remember the BMA chairman claiming that 2006 had been one of the worst years on record for the NHS with all the job losses, training budgets slashed, operations being delayed, hospitals closing, more PFI schemes and the gradual introduction of the private sector into primary care.

The other thing that New Labour did was to lash out loads of money on managers, all on high salaries, all business orientated positions, hardly any of them medical men."

"Have you got anything else to look into now as well?"

"I'm still very interested in what happened at Orgreave, when the miners were given an absolute battering by the police. I remember the BBC spreading lies about what actually happened that day. On the News they showed two clips, the first was one of miners throwing stones at the police, the second was the police charging them. Anybody seeing that would think that is what happened but actually it was the other way round. It was after the police had made a totally unprovoked attack on the miners, that they retaliated. I know that is what happened because a lad from

110

Parr that I know was there and saw it all and then got hit on the back of his head while he was running away."

"Is that all?"

"Not quite. Just two on a personal matter. I want to know why the Council decided to change bin day on our road to a Monday and how Councillor Moore, who was four weeks in arrears with his rent, when I went away, has gone and bought a brand new car!"

Alan spent much of the following morning on the shop floor and so it was almost lunch time before he got back to the drawing office. There he found Jennifer talking, in what he had called the previous day, her calm and collected manner about how Mary had recently discovered a web site that provided a lot of information about some economic thing called financialisation.

"You know what, Jennifer, I just don't know how you two ever find the time to do all the stuff you do at home at night. You are always so busy reading, writing articles, on the phone to each other, you cooking Catalan dishes with your mum and going out jogging three times a week."

"I also go to Bingo every Thursday night as well."

"You spend time every week playing Bingo. I somehow doubt it."

"Well I once went to Stubshaw Cross Labour Club. Highly entertaining in a very quaint sort of way, I thought. Anyway the answer to your question how do I find the time to do all those things is that I only go out jogging twice a week now."

There was no doubt about it. She was a class act and to think that he had initially thought of her as unsuitable for the job that she now excelled at. He remembered at the end of her first week, she had joined them all for their Friday lunchtime drink in the pub and the first thing Dave Morris had said to her was, "Are you Alan's new wife?" and then "What do you do. Do you just make the tea?"

Then there was the time when Horace from Wages had been in the Print Room and had made some reactionary comment along the lines that a woman's place was in the kitchen. Jennifer had loomed up from behind one of the cabinets and said loudly: "Women who want equality with men are guilty of low expectations!" causing Horace to literally flee from the place.

Another thing that Alan remembered about her, had happened a week later when she had a bit of an altercation with Pete Mulholland. Talking about something that was happening in Ashurst on the following Saturday morning, he had said to Alan: "If she's

111

free, I'll bring the wife as well."

Jennifer said to him that she thought that was sexist to describe his wife in that way. Then Cliff said to her: "If she's free on Saturday morning, I'll fetch our Maud as well. Is that all right, Jennifer?"

She thought that it was, assuming that the name of Cliff's wife was Maud. However she later discovered her name was Betty and that in St Helens, it was quite common for a man to refer to his wife as 'our Maud', just like men in West Yorkshire who call their wife 'our lass'.

Later that evening, there was a knock on the door. It was their neighbour Janice with a parcel for Thelma which had been delivered earlier in the day. She then asked if either of them had heard the news about Sutton Manor. They hadn't and so she proceeded to tell them what she had been told earlier in the day by the mother of a young miner who used to work there.

"This sculpture is going to be called 'The Dream'. It will have the shape of the head and neck of a young girl. Her eyes are closed, dreaming both about her future but also about the old colliery and all the people who once worked there and in some cases died there. It is intended to give hope and aspiration for the future and become a positive symbol for the whole area. It will be 20 metres high and will stand on a large replica of the tally that miners always carry underground for their identification, and on a metal plinth that will bear the inscription "Dream Sutton Manor".

"And do you know what, Thelma? If we stand on our tiptoes, we might even be able to see it from our bedroom windows!"

17. Telling Stevo about Uno's Dabs

"It's not even half twelve and here you are sat all on your own in the middle of the day. I thought that you had at least one friend in the world. Clearly you haven't."

It was Les Jackson, another former Wilkinson's draughtsman, who had just walked into the *Ring o' Bells*, bought himself a pint and turned round to see who was in the place.

"It's a one off, Les. I've arranged to meet somebody, but they haven't arrived yet."

"It's not another woman, is it?"

"No, it's another man."

"Well, I could take that one of two ways, I suppose."

"So what are you doing in here in the middle of the day? I thought you were still working at that firm in Bolton."

"Not now. It got closed down. They said I could go and work at their other place if I wanted to. I would have gone but I didn't fancy driving up to Blackburn five times a week."

"So are you still living up Hemsley?"

"No. We've moved to the New Bold estate. The old house we had was fine when there were five of us living there but it was too big for just me and our Maud. So we've sold it, paid off the mortgage, bought a car and just had a week's holiday on the Isle of Man."

"Did you go there in the car?"

"No, we swam it."

"So, do you think you'll enjoy being retired?"

"It hasn't sunk in yet. I can't believe that I was driving to Bolton every day for nearly three years. Good place to work at though, good set of lads and I had a few trips out as well."

"Where did you get to?"

"One of my best jobs was to a steel mill in Romania. I must have gone there at least four times. I also went to Norway twice and Sweden once, but that was only for a day."

"Well, I worked at Wilkinson's for over 50 years. Never got finished once and they have even asked me to carry on working part-time, but I think that is now coming to an end."

"Bloody hell, Alan. You are not still working, are you? You must be well turned 80 by now."

"I'm 68 or maybe 69 but I still can't quite work it out."

"Are you still living in Silkstone Street with Thelma?"

"Yes."

"Any grandkids yet?"

"Three."

"Do you ever see any of the old gang about?"

"I've seen a few of them. Stan Middlehurst has come back from Eastbourne and is living in Vincent Street in St Helens. John Mather lives on his own with his dog in Bolton Street, Phil Bond is living with his son up Nook End and I often see Les Williams but have never spoken to him."

"Why not?"

"Because whenever I do see him, he's always driving the Arriva bus to Warrington, that's why"

"Anybody else?"

"I bumped into Jack Tiplady in Wigan last week. He's living in Horwich now and told me that Janet is now back in her old house in Horace Street in St Helens. Do you remember her?"

"I do. She used to smoke like Top Works chimney, didn't she?"

"Yes, that's the one."

At this point they were joined by Alan's old friend Eric Yates. Stan said 'hello' to him and then 'goodbye' to the pair of them and walked into the bar where he was also hoping to meet someone.

"What do you want, Eric?" said Alan, knowing full well, how slow Eric always was at putting his hand in his pocket. But today things were very different. Eric opened his wallet and showed Alan that it was full of £20 notes.

"I've just had a big win on the gee gees. All had the name of girlfriends I had once had. There was Rose from Gillarsfield, Anne from Widnes, Valerie from Eccleston and Linda from Fingerpost. So I picked Rose's Folly, Queen Anne, Val's Cottage and Lindy Loo in a Yanky. One was at 7 to 1, one was 14 to 1, one was 16 to 1 and one was at 20 to 1. Much to my utter amazement, they all won. I couldn't believe it. So let me buy the ale."

After they talked about what Eric might do with all his winnings and after Eric had bought him another pint, Alan said: "Can I give you some advice, Eric? Let's go and put the rest of that money into your bank account. If it gets round town you have got a bloody fortune in your wallet, you'll be rung up by all your so called old mates, and nearly all of them will be broke and have a good sob

114

story to tell you."

Alan knew what Eric was like, a good bloke to have as a pal, but sometimes a little bit gullible just as he himself had once been when he was still an apprentice at Wilkinson's.

Within half an hour most of that money was in the bank. Then they walked into ASDA, where Eric's shopping included a bottle of brandy and a bottle of Pernod.

"One for you and one for Thelma."

Then he went on to say that he was now going to visit an old pal from Clock Face and a former Ravenhead miner. The man had fallen on really hard times and Eric wanted to help stop him from being thrown out of his house. There were a couple of matters of common interest that Alan had wanted to talk with him about, but that could wait. Eric, now able to help somebody in distress, had to be encouraged and applauded.

Back home, Alan told Thelma about his afternoon. She would always be so pleased that Eric's trickery of sneaking into the Co-op Hall on Christmas Eve in 1962 at Alan's expense, had led to her and Alan getting together. Where would she be now if Eric hadn't behaved so badly that night?

The following day they decided they would have a day out in Huddersfield. There was a very good reason for this. Despite him having been a rugby league fan for over 50 years and having a great interest in the games' history, he had still not yet visited the George Hotel which was where the decision to start the Northern Union had been taken by 21 northern rugby clubs.

They went on the train from Warrington Central and by 11 o'clock they were in the hotel and walking down the steps that led to the Heritage Centre. In front of them was a well-built man in overalls. He walked through the entrance door and then held it open for them. Much to their surprise it was Mike Stephenson, just doing a bit of painting.

On hearing they were Saints fans and on their first visit, he started to give them a guided tour of the place. Soon Alan was telling 'Stevo' about the rivalry in St Helens before the war, between those who followed the Saints and those who followed the Recs and then post war about a local amateur team with the unusual name of Uno's Dabs. Thelma didn't say much at first but as soon as she did speak, Stevo realised that she was Welsh and so began talking about some of the famous players from the Valleys that he had

115

either watched as a boy at Crown Flatts or had later played with or against in both England and Australia.

Then two other interesting characters walked in. One was Sam Morton, who looked after the place, most days of the week, accompanied by the former referee, Billy Thompson, a regular visitor. As a result it was over an hour later before they could get away. After their lunch, they went down to the market. It was there that Alan bought a book about the history of the cotton mills of Oldham. For two pounds it was a bargain if you like that sort of thing. Then came a real stroke of luck when he picked up an old battered leather wallet. Inside it, he found a couple of pamphlets about Italian churches, which were of little interest to him. But lodged between them was what for him was an absolute treasure; something to be savoured later that evening.

On their way back to the railway station, they saw three middle-aged couples in animated conversation among themselves. Alan soon realised that they were talking in French and guessed possibly why they might be there and so he said to them: "Bonjour mes amis, cherchez vous le George Hotel?"

And with that he pointed to the large formidable building about 50 yards away.

"Vous voulez visiter?"

"Oui, c'est possible pour nous?"

And with that he led this group of French treizistes back to the Heritage Centre and introduced them to Sam, Billy and Stevo. Fortunately one of the women spoke a little English and so it was handshakes all round, a couple of kisses and Sam shaking Alan's hand probably for the third time, before they could get away.

A crowded train meant that it was impossible for Alan to look at what was inside the purse that he had bought and so it was later that evening before he was able to see its contents. It was the paperwork associated with a soldier called Arthur Worthington from Burnley, returning home in October 1919. Among the papers were his Soldier's Demobilisation Account, RASC Transfer to Reserve Certificate, Transfer of Payment of Separation Allowance, Allotment of Pay and a receipt for a returned great coat for which he would receive one pound. All were contained in an envelope headed Cover of Certificate and Other Documents of Soldiers on Demobilisation, Transfer to the Reserve or Discharge.

The following Monday Alan and Thelma went shopping in St

116

Helens. As always, they called in to Wardleworths Bookshop to see if there were any new rugby league books on the shelf, but there was nothing there that he did not already have or want.

Back home, there was a message on the phone from Cliff telling Alan that he had gone down with the flu and would be off work for the rest of the week. Could Alan could pick up on the job that he had nearly finished at St Johns Wood sub-station in North London? With Duffy away all week, it would be better than just leaving it until the following Monday for him to decide on it, by which time there would only be four days left for a job that had to be completed by the Friday lunch time of that same week.

What Alan had to do was to go up to Billinge, collect Cliff's keys to his drawers and be told what part of the job Cliff had not yet completed. It was to draw a block cable diagram, add two relays to a panel assembly and check that the changes that he had made to the main fuse board, were still necessary.

Alan spent much of the following morning in the Assembly Shop and only managed to get back to the Drawing Office as everybody else was starting their lunch. It would also be the first time he had spoken with Jennifer as she had been away for much of the previous fortnight recovering from a similar bad dose of flu.

"So what's been happening in the financial world, Jennifer, while you have been away?"

"Quite a lot, Alan, although none of it was any of my fault."

"Well, that's a change" laughed Tariq.

"We are having a bit of a global financial earthquake."

"Go on then. Tell me."

"In January the global stock market, which includes Britain's FTSE, suffered its biggest fall since September 2001. Two weeks later, leaders from the G7 group of industrialised nations said that world-wide losses stemming from the collapse of the US sub-prime mortgage market could reach $400 billion.

Last week one of the most revered name in the finance world admitted that one of its private equity funds could not repay its debt. For every $1 of equity that the $22 billion Carlyle Capital Corporation fund held, was leveraged with $32 of loans. In other words it toppled over under the weight of unsustainable debt.

Then the crisis hit Bear Stearns, another Wall Street investment bank. Last month its shares were trading at $93. Last Thursday they discovered they had less than $3 billion in their possession. It was

117

not enough to open for business the next day. It literally spiralled from being very healthy to practically insolvent in 72 hours and could only survive by being taken over by JP Morgan for $2 a share. In the annals of Wall Street, there had never been such a demise."

"So is all that bad news or very bad news?"

"It's very bad news if you got all your life savings in the Carlyle Capital Corporation."

"Not me. I haven't even been to Carlisle."

She then told him that the next issue of *The Gap* would attempt to cover all these developments although that would not be an easy article for anyone to write. With the way things were moving in the money markets and the banking world, such an article would probably be out of date by the time the magazine had been printed. It would be issue number 10 and with enough material to cover 12 pages, quite an increase from the usual eight.

"So who are writings all these articles. If it is just you and your Mary, you must be staying up very late at night every night."

"Two of our new members in London are pretty good at writing and very keen too, so that helps spread the load around."

"Well, I'll tell you one subject that it might be worth you writing about. It would be about the influence that members of the Bilderberg Group have on world politics. Some of those people earn more in one day than I earn in a year."

"A bit of loose language there, Alan. You should have said some of those get more in one day than you get in a year."

"Always so precise, Jennifer, always so precise. So what can you tell me about this organisation? I know that you have an interesting bunch of neighbours in your street in Bryn, but I don't think that any of them will be members of it."

But before she could respond, Duffy walked in complaining bitterly about the lack of progress on what had now become an urgent job at Cockenzie Power Station in Scotland. It was one that no one in the office knew the faintest thing about because all the information about it was probably still in a folder located in the boss's super-efficient, well organised filing system under lock and key in his office.

18. "Watch your language, young lady"

Everyone in the Drawing Office was busy. Jennifer was working on some complicated meter compensation calculations. Tariq was trying to find space to fit another relay into a cubicle that would soon be going to a cotton mill in Iran. Colin was making a small change to a schematic diagram for Ironbridge Power Station in Shropshire. Cliff was on the phone trying to find out whether the drawings he had posted to a factory in Tunisia a week ago had arrived, and if they had arrived, which issue were they. Alan was drawing a block cable diagram for a factory in Iceland and Shaun was checking a parts list for a job at West Burton.

Suddenly the silence was broken when Jennifer swore, probably because the calculations that she was doing were proving very difficult.

"Watch your language, young lady. There are gentlemen in the room."

"Well if there are any gentlemen in the room, I can't see any of them. And if there were any gentleman here, one of them would have offered to help me with these very difficult calculations."

"Jennifer, you are the world's expert on meter compensation calculations. How could any of us lesser mortals help you?"

Silence reigned for quite a while until she shouted out: "I've finished it. I am even cleverer than I thought I was."

"Let's celebrate it. Anyway it's your turn to put the kettle on."

A few minutes later she came in from the kitchen with tea and coffee for them all and then asked Cliff a rather unusual question: "Cliff, how can you watch your language? You can speak a language, you can study a language, you can translate a language, you can even study the history of a language but how can you watch a language?"

"Nice one Jennifer. Whenever it comes to the use or misuse of words you always have something interesting to say."

"Thank you, Alan."

"And to think that you could not even speak proper English like us lot do in Ashurst until tha wuz turned 22."

"Thank you again, Alan."

Then it was Cliff's turn: "Jennifer do they teach English as a foreign language up in Geordie land?"

119

"How many times do I have to tell you that I don't come from Geordie land? I'm a Mackem from the world famous city of Sunderland."

"Sorry about that Jennifer. So can I ask you if they teach English as a foreign language in Sunderland?"

"If you had had anything like a decent education Cliff, you should have asked whether English was taught as a foreign language in Sunderland. The use of the word 'they' in that question is poor English, though I don't suppose you would or could appreciate that."

"Well, actually I had a very good education. That is because I went to one of the top public schools in the North of England."

Tariq looked up in amazement and said: "Which one was that, Cliff? And if you did go to a public school, how come you finished up here, working as a draughtsman?"

"It was because the public school that I went to was the Knowsley Road Junior School in St Helens. It was where the public of the Newtown district of the town sent their children."

"He not only learned to read and write and do mental arithmetic there, you know" laughed Alan. "He also learned how to read out loud from his paper to a very uninterested audience."

Cliff was well known in the office for reading out loud bits of his paper every lunchtime, to whoever had the misfortune to be sat near to him.

"I'll tell you one thing about Knowsley Road School. I bet there is no other school in the whole of England and Wales that has produced as many pupils who went on to become famous for writing about rugby league."

"Who then?" asked Colin.

"Off the top of my head there's Alex Service, Ray French, Roger Grime, Ray Gent, Phil Howard and Alan Tucker. They all went there at one time or another."

"That's only six of them."

"You tell me another school in the North of England that has produced more than six."

"There's bound to be one in Wigan. I'll find out and let you know."

"I'll tell you summat else too that you won't believe. St Helens is the town that has produced the greatest number of rugby league writers."

120

"Who?"

"On top of those six, there's Mike Critchley, Mike Appleton, Keith Macklin, Andrew Quirke, Dennis Whittle, Peter Cropper, John Vose, and also worth knowing is the fact that the *Rugby Leaguer* was first written and published in the town."

"Have any famous players gone there?"

"Ray French is the only one that I can think of."

"Have there ever been any famous writers who came from Ashurst?" asked Jennifer.

"There was Les Earnshaw for a start. He wrote three novels. His best one was *The Actress went to Paradise*. He even got interviewed by David Frost on TV once. It was hilarious. He also wrote stuff for *Brookside* and *The Bill*. And then there was that Welsh lad Tommy Evans, who worked in the Paint Shop. He was the secretary of the Ashurst Rugby League Supporters' Association and used to write a fanzine called *The Dropped Ball*."

"Can I ask you a question, Jennifer, as you are no doubt the most widely read person in here?"

"Whether I say 'yes' or 'no' Cliff, you'll probably ask it anyway. Go on then."

"How many languages are there in the world today?"

"Around 7,000 languages are spoken, but only about 10 percent of them are spoken by more than 100,000 people."

"How do you know all that?"

"When I was at Salford University I was very friendly with a student from the Orkney Isles who was studying linguistics."

"What's all that about?"

"Linguistics is all to do with the nature of language and the communication between people. It deals with the study of different languages and the search for things that are common to all languages and groups of languages."

"And you learned all that in Salford, well I am amazed."

"Well then, I'll surprise you a bit more then by telling you that linguistics can be broken down into five sub areas: phonetics – the study of the production of speech sounds, morphology which is the structure of words, syntax is the structure of sentences and pragmatics but I can't remember what the fifth one is."

"Sounds rather boring to me."

"I bet you can't tell us which are the six most used languages In the world."

121

"I could try, Cliff."

"Go on then."

"Mandarin, Spanish, English, Hindi, Arabic and Portuguese. Is that correct?"

"Knowing you Jennifer, it probably is."

"Well you will all be pretty pleased to know that I passed my GCE in Latin."

It was Alan now keen to get in on the act:

"I bet that comes in handy for drawing a block cable diagram."

"Well I found it very useful when I was at that big textile exhibition in Argentina, which for those who don't know much about geography, is in Latin America."

"Go on then. Say something in Latin for us, Greeno."

"How about my declining a noun for you: Bellum, bellum, bellum, belli, bello, bella."

"What the heck is that?"

"That's the nominative, vocative, accusative, genitive, dative and ablative cases of the noun bellum which, as you will all know is the Latin word for war which accounts for the English words bellicose and belligerent"

"Greeno, you really are an absolute genius."

"Would you like me to conjugate the verb to love?"

Silence.

"Amo, amas, amat, amamus, amatis, amant."

"That was all in the present tense. I can also do it in the future, perfect, pluperfect, past historic and imperfect tenses."

"What use is all that? No wonder they all stopped talking in Latin."

"We have all those aspects of language in English, you know."

"Not in Wigan they don't" laughed Colin, "and I bet they don't have 'em in Sunderland either, do they Jennifer?"

Then Alan casually mentioned that verbs could exist in one of four moods: indicative, imperative, subjunctive and infinitive.

"If you carry on any longer like this Greeno, you will put me into a very bad mood."

It was Colin's contribution to the 'lecture', but before any more could be said, the fire alarms went off and so everybody grabbed their jackets and headed for the exit. But it was literally a false alarm and so back in the office 10 minutes later, everybody decided that working on the design of electrical control systems might be a

122

lot more interesting than listening to 'Greeno' talking in a dead language while he was still just about half alive.

When he arrived home a couple of hours later he was greeted with the news that Josh and Joanna were in the back garden. Their parents had gone to visit a neighbour who was in hospital following an accident that he had recently been involved in, at a children's clothing shop in Manchester.

"That's annoying. I have been looking forward all day to you showing me how to use the hoover and the washing machine, but I suppose I had better stick to what you know I am very good at."

"And what might that be? Please remind me."

"Playing Ludo, Animals, Snap and Draughts."

"Well, we'll have our tea first and then we can play those games or do whatever the two of them want."

An hour or so passed in this very pleasant way and then Neil and Rebecca arrived with an account of how a 25 year old, 15 stone six foot two inch tall man who had played in the front row for Ashurst Hornets for the last four years could be involved in an accident in a Mothercare shop.

The accident was quite simple to describe. It could easily have happened in the turbine hall of a power station, or in the mixing room of a chemical works or in the machine shop of a glass works but surely never in a children's clothing store. But before more could be said about it, their next door neighbour Phil knocked on the door, wanting to borrow Alan's electric drill. As he did, Neil, Rebecca and the children left. When they had gone Phil went on to tell Alan that he had just heard some very sad news. It was the death of the former Wigan centre Eric Ashton at the age of 73.

Although they were both keen Saints fans, the two of them could both appreciate good rugby being played, irrespective of who by. One pair of players that Alan had always enjoyed watching, was Eric Ashton as centre to the Welsh winger Billy Boston. Eric was St Helens born and bred, but had never made it into his home town team, despite living less than a mile from their Knowsley Road ground. And Cliff would no doubt be also saddened by the news because he used to live in Mulberry Avenue and had known Eric quite well.

Being a rugby league fan was a lot like being part of a large family with relatives all over the world. And so because there were so many people in this family, both supporters and players alike,

123

their passing into another world from this one was happening all the time. And so it was with the death of Eric Ashton.

Whenever Alan heard any Saints fans say that they hated Wigan, well he just had to mention Eric's name to show how stupid they were, to say that. And whenever he heard people say something bad about the Welsh or people with a different coloured skin, he would just mention the name of Billy Boston. This was a very simple way to attack stupid comments made about people from other towns or other countries and who were much respected all across the world.

Like many other Saints fans must surely have done over the years, Alan had often wondered what a partnership of Tom van Vollenhoven and Eric Ashton would have been like. It would have to be very good though to beat any partnership of Vol with either Duggie Greenall or Ken Large.

The following lunchtime found Cliff keen to know more about the English language that he had been using every day for the last 60 odd years. Like many people who had grown up in South Lancashire, he was well aware of the deliberate misuse of words, like when Stan Middlehurst told them that he was returning north, but would not have his name put on the Ashurst electrical register when he actually meant electoral register.

He also remembered their tea lady, Joan, back in the 1960s. At the time the firm was manufacturing equipment for the electrification of the railway line between Manchester and Crewe. One day she had come into the office with her trolley and announced that she had just heard that the firm had won a big order for some elocution equipment.

He told Jennifer about this casually and not surprisingly she had more than a few words to say on the matter. It was all to do with the noble art of punning. She then proceeded to explain   that this could be described as a play on words, in which a humorous effect is produced by using a word that suggests two or more meanings or by exploiting similar sounding words having different meanings or using words that have several meanings. Then she proceeded to give them a few examples: "I was struggling to figure out how lightening works and then suddenly it struck me.

Yesterday I held the door open for a clown. I thought it was a nice jester.

Atheism is a non-prophet institution.

A pessimist's blood type is usually B negative.

Every calendar's days are numbered.

No matter how much you move an envelope it will still be stationery."

Then she asked him if he had ever heard of Spoonerism. He had, but he didn't know what it was and neither had he ever heard of the Reverend William Archibald Spooner.

She then told them that he was a tutor at Oxford University who 'enjoyed' a certain notoriety among his students and fellow dons, as a result of his nervous conditions which often led him to mix up his words, producing comic or absurd effects. For example, once when telling off a student who rarely attended his classes, Spooner was alleged to have said to him that: "You have hissed all of my mystery lectures".

Another time he had met someone whom he had briefly known in the past and is believed to have said "I remember your name perfectly, but I just cannot think of your face". His best one though occurred when he was discussing religion and was reputed to have said "The Lord is a shoving leopard" while another was about his friend who he said went to work on a well boiled icicle by which he actually meant a well-oiled bicycle.

Then Alan chipped in to say his favourite wordsmith was Tommy Cooper and proceeded to quote three of his favourites: "I went to buy some camouflage trousers but I couldn't see any in the shop.

I'm on a whisky diet. I've lost three days already.

I saw the doctor yesterday and asked him if he had anything for wind and he gave me a kite."

Then it was Colin's turn. One of his favourite character for misusing words was the American sex symbol Mae West: "Save a boyfriend for a rainy day and another in case it doesn't rain.

I generally avoid temptation unless I can't resist it.

It is better to be looked over than overlooked."

Then Tariq said that Groucho Marx was his favourite, quoting three of his best known ones: "Women should be obscene and not heard.

Please accept my resignation. I don't want to belong to any club that will accept me as a member.

I never forget a face but in your case I'll be glad to make an exception."

Then he quoted a few quips from Billy Connolly.

"Why should I learn algebra. I'm never likely to go there.
A well balanced man has a drink in both hands
Why do people say that their eyes are not what they used to be?
So what did they used to be, ears or Wellington boots?"

Always one to finish off a good conversation as well as start one, Jennifer said that just before he passed away, Groucho had come out with one of his most memorable quotes: "Why should I care about posterity? What's posterity ever done for me?"

Then she went on to say that not many people appreciated that William Shakespeare was pretty big on this clever use and misuse of words, although it is generally believed that he always described them as mixed phrases.

"Jennifer, following your time at Salford University studying electrical engineering and picking up an enormous amount of knowledge about the English language, did you ever find the time to learn a foreign language?"

"Yes, I did and am still quite fluent in both French and Belgian."

"And how useful is it to be tri-lingual, living in Bryn and working in Ashurst?"

She then proceeded to tell him of the advantages of being able to speak a second language. They included helping delay the chance of Alzheimer's and dementia by as much as five years. It was because the parts of the brain that are strengthened while speaking other languages included not just the analytical and logical side of the brain, but the emotional and social side as well. It was caused by making the grey matter in the brain work harder.

"That certainly seems to make sense to me" replied Cliff.

"My next door neighbour Tom is turned 90. He plays tennis once a week, walks half a mile to get his paper every day and speaks Esperanto like a native."

"Aye, like a native of Billinge," Alan was heard to mutter.

19. "Your mother grew up in Tiger Bay"

It was Thursday, but both Joanna and Josh were not at school. Work was being carried out on the roof and so the whole building was closed for the day. Rebecca had brought the children round and then gone to visit her friend Sally who was currently at home in Nutgrove recovering from an operation on her knee.

The first thing Thelma did was take them both into the back garden to show them what had been growing over the last fortnight. Then they all went back into the house, Thelma brought out some of her famous Welsh scones that she had just baked and as they were eating them, Joanna said: "Granma, one of my friends doesn't come to our school anymore."

"Who was that?"

"Tracey and her sister doesn't come any more as well. She was in another class."

"Have they gone to another school?"

Joanna hunched her shoulders, her way of indicating that she didn't know.

Later Thelma heard from Rebecca why Tracey and her sister Mandy had left. Her father worked as a joiner on building sites all over Merseyside. He was also a strong trade unionist, always keen to make sure that all the sites that he worked on, were safe. For this 'crime', he had been blacklisted by the employers' organisation and could no longer find work right across the North West. As a result he had been forced to take his family back to Motherwell in Scotland to live with his widowed sister and hopefully find work there and make a fresh start to their life.

A few nights later Alan and Thelma were sitting in the kitchen discussing what to do for the rest of the evening. It was nice enough to go bowling, but then into the room came Megan with Daisy. Straight away any such plans were shelved as grandmother duties took over. With the little one gently placed on Granma's lap, Megan announced that she had come with some fantastic news that she had just received from her friend Ann.

Ann lived in Cardiff, and had been friends with Megan ever since they had first met at Coventry University. After graduating, they had kept in contact, usually through the internet. When she had started researching Thelma's background, Megan had made little progress and so she had contacted Ann to see if she could help. Then right out of the blue, Ann rang Megan and now Megan was here to tell Thelma what Ann had told her.

"You remember that I sent Ann all the details you had given me about your mother's name, her address in Tonyrefail and the fact that she was in the Women's Land Army during the war. Well it was that last thing that really helped Ann. This was because she had an aunt who had also been in the Land Army. Ann had always kept in contact with her, even more so now because she was losing her eye sight and had recently gone to live in a care home a few miles away.

Last week Ann asked her aunt if she could remember the names of any of the girls from those times. There was Margaret who married an Australian soldier and went to live in Adelaide, Denise who returned to Newtown and married a farmer, Pat who went to work in a bakery in Neath, Barbara who became a nurse in Port Talbot and Becci who died in 1944 a few months after she had given birth to a little baby girl."

Thelma froze.

"I asked her to tell me about Becci. She said that the two of them had been good friends. Becci's full name was Rebecca Linda Johnson. She had grown up in the Tiger Bay district of Cardiff and had a boyfriend who was a sailor. She was a good swimmer and had once rescued a child who had fallen into a river. She was a bit on the short side, quite strong and one of her most distinguishing features was that she had freckles all over her body."

Then Megan took a DVD out of her handbag, gave it to Alan and told Thelma listen to what Ann had recorded. It was her aunt's exact description of what she knew about Thelma's mother. It was such a moving tale.

"One day Becci told us all that she was going to have a baby. It was in the spring of 1944. Her boyfriend was a Greek seaman although sadly a few weeks earlier his ship had left port, but he had said to her that when he returned, he wanted them to get married. Unfortunately his ship went down and he never came back. Sometime later Becci had a little baby girl. It was a lovely little thing. Me and some of the other girls used to visit her quite a lot, but by then I was working on another farm about 10 miles away and didn't get the chance to see her as much as I would have liked to. Then came that terrible day when she lost her life.

"It was quite a nice day and Becci left the baby in its pram in

128

the yard. Well it wasn't a pram really, more like a wooden box on wheels, but then Becci was always good at making things. She didn't expect to be away long and was sure the baby would be quite safe. But things didn't turn out like she had intended. She had done her shopping and was coming home. As she crossed the road, she had been knocked over by a man on a motor bike. By the time an ambulance had arrived, she had passed away and at the time, nobody knew anything about her baby and where it was.

It was still in the yard and then it started raining. Luckily the next door neighbour must have heard the baby crying. She took it into her house, thinking that Becci would soon return from where ever she had gone to. But of course she never came back. The neighbour looked after it for a couple of days and then it was taken away by a man from the council. No one ever saw it again. It was a lovely little thing. I loved to hold it and play with it."

That was just how the aunt had told Ann, who then went on to tell her that the little baby had survived the incident and was now living in Lancashire and the mother of two children and three grandchildren.

Then Megan said that there was more interesting news: "Last week Ann did some more research based on what her aunt had told her. She found a family called Johnson living in Angelina Street in Tiger Bay in the 1930s. There was a mother, father, two boys John and Brian and a girl called Rebecca Linda.

She also discovered that close by there was South Church Street school which Becci would almost certainly have gone to. When she started trying to find out if there were any school records about, she discovered that quite a few famous people had once gone to this school."

"Who?"

"There was Joe Erskine the boxer, another was Shirley Bassey the singer and there were two men who became famous rugby players. One was Johnny Freeman and the other was Billy Boston, who I am sure Alan will know about."

"Do you know him, Alan?" asked Thelma.

"I don't know him personally, but I do know how old he probably is now and I also know that he came from a large family. So there's a fair chance that she might have been in the same class as him or some of his other brothers or sisters."

"Is there any way you could contact him?"

129

"Possibly. I have a pal in Wigan who knows him quite well. I'll ring Ron later. I'm sure I've got his number somewhere."

Then Thelma said out loud: "I was born in the summer of 1944. My mother was born in May 1924 so she would have been about 20 when she had me. I wonder why and when she moved to Tonyrefail because that is where I was born. It is what was written on my birth certificate."

Then she turned back to Megan and asked if Ann's aunt had said anything else.

It turned out that the aunt had asked Ann why she was asking all these questions and so Ann was able to tell her what had happened to Becci's baby. It brought tears to her aunt's eyes. She then lent Ann a group photograph of all the Land Army girls from the area and the aunt had pointed out which one was Becci.

"What is Ann going to do with it all?"

"She is going to get copies made and post them up to me."

"Thanks for all that, Megan."

Before Thelma could say much more, Daisy made the sort of noises that indicated that she was now filling her nappy. Megan took her up to the bathroom, did what she had to do and on coming downstairs decided it was time to take the little one home.

"She'll be wanting her feed in half an hour. I'll just have time to get it made. She's as regular as clockwork, the little darling."

"Well, don't ever leave her in the yard whenever you go out shopping."

Megan laughed, held up the baby for Granma to give her a big sloppy kiss and then left.

"Alan, after all that, I think I need a strong drink. Have we got any Pernod left?"

Half an hour later Thelma had just about recovered from the effects of Megan's visit. They decided there was still time to go bowling, although after finishing what was in the bottle, Thelma would now have a good reason to explain why she wouldn't bowl very well tonight.

As they were walking to the park, Thelma asked: "Have you done any more work on your Dad's side of the family, Alan?"

"Yes. I did do a bit more last week. But I didn't say anything to you about it because it's taken me a bit of time to get over the shock of what I have found out about him."

"What do you mean?"

130

"You always thought I was a true blue Englishmen."

"Most people round here would probably consider you more of a true red Englishman."

"Well. It's not true."

"How come?"

"I am actually of Dutch extraction."

"How do you make that out?"

"Because I checked up again and discovered that my Dad was born in Upholland."

"That old one again."

"I know that around the time he met my mum, he was working at Triplex in St Helens and lived quite near in Alder Hey Road. He had two brothers. One drowned at Dunkirk and one was killed crossing the Rhine in 1944 around the same time as my Dad was killed at Monte Cassino.

"I also know that his mother was a dinner lady at Knowsley Road School and his father worked at the Daglish Iron Foundry for much of his life. I think after hearing what you have just discovered I will start doing some more research on his family."

Then he asked Thelma if what she had just heard from Megan had affected her, for she had gone very quiet.

"A little bit. When you hear about people who you are related to, it makes the past come alive for me, hearing about what they did during their lives many years ago."

"Just imagine this, Thelma. Suppose your mum hadn't died and your dad came back from the war, they got married and you were brought up in Tonyrefail. In one way that might have been very good but then looked at in a different way it might not have been that good. You would never have met and lived with Granny and Grandad, you would never have got interested in Rugby League, you would never have met Charlie, Yorky, Mick, Big Joan, Rita, Hazel and you would never have met me. If you had married some Welsh bloke well you might never have had two children like Rebecca and Robert and you would never have enjoyed eating a Babby's Yed, a split and fish or enjoyed playing Crown Green bowls in Victoria Park and watching the Saints every other week."

Before she could reply they were in the little hut where old Monty was handing out the bowls. Much to their surprise Mr and Mrs Leyland were in there as well. Once they had been their neighbours in Beswick Street. He used to work underground at Parkside Colliery

131

and she had been a cook in Mather's canteen. He had always been a pretty fit bloke, but now walked with a bad limp. It wasn't as a result of an accident in the bowels of the earth though, but from a savage blow to his knee by a police baton at the Orgreave coking plant in South Yorkshire in 1984 during the miners' strike.

His hatred for the man who had done that to him was huge as was his attitude to all those boys in blue who had fought them there. Strangely though, his eldest lad had joined the police force in the late 1970s and was still close to both his parents. In fact it was due to his generosity that his parents had not been forced to sell their house at the end of the strike in 1985 at a time when they were almost penniless.

Frank was slightly older than Alan and was now an active member of the National Pensioners Convention, whose aim and purpose was to deal with the growing number of issues facing the over-65s. Like Alan's son-in-law Neil, he had also been active in his local Labour Party branch, but no longer.

"Don't mention Tony Blair, Margaret Thatcher or Frank Delaney to him" John's wife Doris said to Alan, as they walked across the green but out of hearing by her husband.

"If any of them three ever step foot into Ashurst, they'll finish up in a wooden box and I'm not kidding."

Back in work the following lunch time, Alan was telling Cliff and Jennifer about what Megan had discovered about Thelma's family background and then his joke about being Dutch because one of his parents had been born at Upholland.

Then Cliff spoke about his own wife's interest in the background of members of her family: "Our Maud has been working on her family tree for a while now. She always thought that she was as English as anyone can be. Both her parents grew up in Duncan Street, one set of her grandparents lived at the top of Croppers Hill, the other pair lived at Fingerpost and it was not until as far back as 1798 that one of the relatives could not be said to be truly local. It was her great great great grandfather who had been born in Belgium. Now why would a man come all the way from Belgium to live in St Helens?"

"Maybe it was because he had heard that Burchalls had just opened up a pie shop in Westfield Street!"

"What about you Jennifer. I suppose all your ancestors were Vikings and came across here in a big rowing boat."

"They wouldn't have on my real mother's side because she was born in Barcelona in 1938, as you well know. On my dad's side, most of his family came from near Sunderland but he did have a cousin who really was a Viking because he grew up in Widnes."

At this point Cliff received a phone call, to tell him that a large box had just been delivered to Reception for him. As he left, Jennifer started to tell Alan about what was being planned for the next issue of *The Gap*. It would include an article proving that Gordon Brown was either incompetent or just not very good at Maths. It was based on seven letters all grouped together in an article in a recent copy of *The Guardian* under the heading "Poor show by Labour on Tax".

A year ago, the government had abolished the 10p tax band, something which would apply to the 2008–09 tax year which had just started. In one letter a woman from London had written on how five million people on low incomes would be negatively affected, how none of the MPs had done anything about it and how Labour had just lost her vote. Another was from a woman in Darwen who included details about her income as a part-time worker and how she would be around £150 a year worse off.

This had led Jennifer visiting one of her neighbours, who also worked part-time and had now discovered that she would be worse off by almost £100. She also reminded Jennifer how Labour had lost many supporters a couple of years earlier when they had raised the state pension by a miserly 75 pence a week. All this and more examples of other low paid neighbours who were going to be affected soon convinced Jennifer that she should write an article about it for the next issue of *The Gap.*

Alan's immediate response was to say that the next day he was in work he would show the article to John Carter and ask him what he thought about it.

20. The Church of the Everyday Saints

"Who was that at the door?" asked Thelma as she walked into the living room from the kitchen.

"The Church of the Latter Day Saints."

"You were there with them for quite a long time. Have you gone and joined them?"

"No. I told them that I was a member of the Church of the Everyday Saints, which sort of baffled them a little bit."

"I bet it did and I suppose you came out with that old faithful comment of yours about Man creating God in his own image."

"I always do to any religious fundamentalist I have the pleasure of talking to. It makes sense to me just like it made sense to Louis Feuerbach back in 1880 or whenever he wrote it."

"To be honest Alan, I think that some of the things that your Mr Feuerbach originally wrote, got slightly misinterpreted."

"Why. Have you read it in the German?"

"Not yet, but I have heard that after he wrote it, it was first translated into French and then into English by an Italian linguist."

"How do you know that?"

"Mrs Bottomley told me last Thursday while we were waiting to get served in the butcher's."

"And how does she know that?"

"Her husband told her, just before he died."

"That must be over 20 years ago."

"Well she's got a good memory. Anyway what else of little value did you tell them?"

"I told them to be very careful for their lives if they ever go knocking on doors in Wigan."

"Why is that?"

"Because a lot of people in Wigan don't like the Saints."

"Did they understand what you were on about?"

"Probably not. They were both Americans and they probably won't understand our Ashurst sense of humour."

Then she changed the subject and continued: "I haven't had much chance to make any tea for you. I've been on the phone half the afternoon answering all your phone calls."

"So who's rung me then?"

"Jennifer for a start. You promised her you would write an article for her magazine and she wants it done by Sunday."

"I've done half of it already. Two mores lines and it'll be finished. Who else has rung?"

"Cliff. His neighbour died last week and the man's daughter has found a load of old programmes that she wants to go to a good home."

"Great."

"Somebody called Keith rang from the Rugby League Heritage Centre in Huddersfield. He's going to ring back tomorrow."

"OK."

The following day Alan was in the Drawing Office, wondering why Duffy had asked him to come into work. There were three others in there with him, Cliff, Jennifer and Tariq and none of them seemed to have much to do.

Jennifer unwrapped a chocolate biscuit, started to eat it and at the same time threw the paper wrapping right into the wastepaper bin, about six yards away.

"Looks as though you have been practising again."

"Unlike you, Cliff."

"I don't eat chocolate biscuits, so I don't need to."

Alan sat there listening to them and thinking what a contribution she had made to the office, both on the technical side and socially. He remembered well the day he had interviewed her. It had started quite badly for her. She arrived late and answered his first two questions incorrectly. But as the interview had gone on, she sort of relaxed, almost as though she knew that she had blown it. But she hadn't. There was just something about her that Alan liked and the other three people he had seen for the vacancy were all young men who had not impressed him. So he took a bit of a gamble, employing a woman in an all-male drawing office.

Not that he was in any way prejudiced against women, though. If he had been, then what would his wife, his mother, his granny, his auntie Doris, his auntie Kitty, his daughter Rebecca, Janice next door, Yorky's widow Joyce and little Joanna have all thought about him. All were female, all had been or still were a pleasure to have known and worked or lived with. So he had offered her the job and by the end of her first week, he realised she was going to be a very welcome addition to the office.

Over the years other women had worked with him, but none had been as good, skilled and knowledgeable as she was. The first one

135

he could remember was Joan, the tea lady from Leigh, always getting her words wrong, but always a source of information about the various scandals that other people in the factory were involved in. Then there was Big Joan who ran the Print Room. A big Saints fan was Joan, all 14 stone of her, unlike her sidekick Rita, who was probably no more than eight stone, and forever with a cigarette in her mouth. The last he had heard about her was that she was now suffering with throat cancer and living in a care home in Southport.

Then there had been Hazel, their former tea girl who had gone to Bradford College, trained to become a teacher and was now the head of a school in Warrington. He also remembered Nancy the Never, so called because whenever she appeared with her trolley, she never had any stories to tell, never had any change and never stayed a minute longer than was necessary.

As he sat there thinking about them all, he also remembered Mrs Foster who had been his very first teacher at Lane Head School and how she used to read stories to the class about a big pink elephant called Rufus.

Finally Duffy appeared, took Alan into his office and told him that Amsterdam were thinking of inviting him to work on a major project that would involve him spending time in Indonesia. There was no need for an immediate answer, certainly not before the details of the job had been seen by both of them. Alan could have said he wasn't interested, but decided to say nothing.

A couple of days later he found himself walking out of Headingley, having just watched the Saints beat Leeds 26–12. He had only decided to go late that afternoon and with his car in Canal Street Garage, he had gone on one of Hatton's coaches. As he walked over the railway bridge towards where all the Saints coaches were parked, he saw a familiar face. It was Glen Delaney, a real blast from the past.

The two of them had often worked together at various power stations, the last one though being 20 years ago now. It was on National Power's Final Metering Scheme and around the time that the Thatcher government had privatised the CEGB and when three new companies: National Power, National Grid and Power Gen had been created. And it had been in the Meter Room at Eggborough Power Station that that they had spent almost a whole week together sorting out all the changes that were called for.

"Hi ya Glen. What are you doing over here?"

136

"I've been watching the Saints. What have you been doing over here? Train spotting?"

As they walked towards where all the St Helens coaches were parked Alan asked Glen whose coach he had come on.

"I didn't come on a coach. I got a lift here with a lad who lives in Bramley."

"So how are you going to get home?"

"With someone telling me there's a spare seat on their coach."

Luckily Alan's coach was not full and Alan distracted the driver's attention as the pair of them got on, not that he would have bothered, although you never know.

The two of them had first met while studying for their ONC at Ashurst Tech and then for their HNC in Electrical Engineering at St Helens Tech. In those days, the one thing Alan remembered about Glen was the way how everything in his life had changed when he had spent nearly all his holiday helping a young widow.

Sally lived then with her two small children in a terraced house in Ashcroft Street and with winter approaching, her house had no lighting or heating due to some faulty electrical wiring. She was also the sister of one of Glen's friends who, a couple of years earlier, had been killed in a car crash on the East Lancs Road near Haydock. Glen had just returned from working at a water treatment plant in Holland and had two weeks holiday to enjoy before going to his next job which would be at a cotton mill in Tunisia.

On hearing of her plight, he had then spent all his holiday rewiring her house and putting new floorboards and a sink in her kitchen. Some of the equipment had been paid for with what he had won in Land's bookmakers the previous day, but the rest of it had come from his own pocket, although at the time she did not know that. By the time his 'holiday' was over, he had not only fallen in love with her, his heart had also gone out to her two children Liam and Cheryl. Not long after they became one big happy family.

"Who are you working for now, Glen?

"I've got my own business, you might be surprised to hear. Anything electrical, house rewires, motor rewires, showers installed etc. I've got Liam working for me and a young black kid off the Brunswick estate who I am giving a bit of a chance to."

"So you've joined the ranks of the capitalist class, have you?"

"You've never changed, have you, Greeno?"

"No, have you?"

137

"Actually no. I now sell my labour power to myself. I am no longer just a number for some multimillion pound corporate business conglomerate that would be ripping me off for every hour I work for them."

"And how's Sally doing?"

"Didn't you know, Alan? I'm very sorry to tell you this, but she is no longer with us. She died three months ago."

"God, I'm sorry to hear that, Glenn. What can I say? What was it?"

"Cancer. She had been suffering with it for a long time. Still we had something like 25 great years together what with her two kids and then our grandchildren. Do you know what, the best thing that I ever did in my whole life was spending two weeks doing up that little terraced house she had in Ashcroft Street."

"What's Cheryl doing? Is she married yet?"

"No, but her and her partner have got two kids. He is a lovely bloke. Frank they call him and as far as I can see there's only one thing wrong with him."

"What's that?"

"He follows Wigan. So, how's Thelma? I know you two are still married because Jack Bolton told me so last Monday. I often see him around town now that he's back living in Hamer Street."

"What about Liam?"

"He's fine. He's a bit of a whizz kid on computers, but at the same time he can still get stuck in to any ordinary wiring jobs that I give him."

They talked about the game they had just watched and other games they seen recently. Then their conversation moved on to power stations they had both once worked at, sometimes together. They included Fiddler's Ferry, Agecroft, Bold, Kearsley, Padiham and Westwood all in Lancashire along with Blyth, Ferrybridge, Rugeley, Thorpe Marsh and West Burton. Time flew and soon they were back in Ashurst. The first stop was the Black Bull where Glen got off, promising to ring Alan soon. Ten minutes later he was sitting in his favourite chair and ready to eat. Then he would no doubt be enticed back to the chess board to try and prevent another defeat.

But before that could start, as usual whenever she had been in town earlier in the day, Thelma had met someone and so had a tale to tell him about. This time it was their old friend Ray.

A few weeks earlier Ray had been in his front garden and seen

138

one of his neighbours from the opposite end of Rivington Lane struggling along, carrying two heavy bags of shopping and looking quite poorly. He had taken the bags off her and invited her to come into the house and sit down. As she sat there, he had even considered ringing for an ambulance, but she insisted she would be all right, if he would just ring her sister and get her to bring some tablets that were on a table by her bed.

Within 10 minutes the sister arrived and immediately started fussing, while thanking Ray for what he had done. As he listened to her talk, Ray had assumed that if she was Ashurst born and bred she must have lived on the other side of the world for a long time because she sounded more like an Aussie.

Then she turned round, looked Ray in the face and said:

"You went to St Luke's school, didn't you? You sat behind me in Miss Jenkins class, and kept pulling my pony tail."

Ray thought about those long time ago happy days at St Luke's. Yes, it was true he had kept annoying the girl sat at the desk in front of him, by pulling her hair. He had never seen her since, probably because around the time they were about to leave junior school, her family had moved to Eccleston on the far side of St Helens. On passing her 11 plus, she had gone to Cowley Girls School. After that she worked for two years in the Wages Office at Pilkington's glass works in St Helens, but meeting an Aussie called Wayne had led to her going to live with him in Brisbane for the next 40 odd years, until he had died and she had decided to come back to England.

Soon the older sister had decided she was well enough to go home but with Ray driving them both the short distance there. There he discovered that Jeanne had only been back in England for less than a month and was still unsure whether she wanted to stay. He offered to drive her round and show her some of the many changes that had been made while she had been away. By the end of the month she had decided she would like to stay in Ashurst and live in a house on Rivington Lane too, but not with her sister at number 117 but with Ray at number 17.

A couple of evenings later the four of them were sat in the Greenall's front room and it soon became clear that her arrival on the scene would be good news all round. It even started off with reference being made to a coincidence, something that Alan always enjoyed hearing about. As soon as Thelma started talking, Jeanne

139

said that she reminded her of one of her friends in Brisbane. This friend also came from South Wales but Jeanne could not quite remember where exactly. Alan produced a map and soon after, Jeanne was sure that the place where her friend came from, was Llantrisant. This was a town about halfway between Tonyrefail where Thelma was born and Cardiff where she had grown up.

Not knowing much about what had happened in Ashurst or anywhere else in England since 1956, Jeanne could not initially appreciate what Ray was doing with all his investigations, although she certainly agreed with people in Britain, campaigning against the privatisation of their National Health Service. One of her big interests in life though was painting, another bit of a coincidence, bearing in mind that was the great pastime of the Greenalls' next door neighbour.

A week later Thelma took Jeanne next door to meet Janice. On hearing that she had once lived in Eccleston, Janice asked her if she had ever seen any paintings by a woman called Margaret Chapman. Jeanne hadn't, but then Janice went on to say that before she was married, and so probably while Jeanne was also living in Eccleston, her name was Margaret Duxberry.

That was a name familiar to Jeanne, as someone that she vaguely remembered from Cowley Girl's school. Sadly though after googling her name on the internet Jeanne discovered that Margaret Chapman had died in 2000.

Jeanne also learned from browsing the internet, that Margaret Chapman had once had a great uncle called Charles Lightoller, who was famous for the fact that he had been the second officer on the Titanic and was a survivor of that terrible tragedy

And even more interestingly, searching around on the internet a few days later, Ray discovered that the curved glass dome that had hung in the ballroom of the Titanic had been made not very far away from his house. It was at a firm called Gardner and Newton who had once been based in Hall Street, right in the middle of St Helens.

21. "I hope that Guy Fawkes is standing"

"I see there is a by-election coming up soon."

"I hope that Guy Fawkes is standing. He's the only one that I would ever consider voting for."

"Well, I must say that he would be dead suited for the job."

"Might smell a bit though."

"Nobody has been round to see me about it or give me some posters to put in my waste paper bin."

"Where do you live, Colin?"

"High Street in Newton le Willows."

"Well, the by-election is near Hull."

"I might be a little bit interested in politics, but I am not going all that way to vote."

"It's in Hull did you say, Alan. It all sounds a bit fishy to me."

"It's not a bad plaice to have an election."

"No codding!"

"They used to have a power station in Hull. I went there once. In fact I went there twice."

"Why. Did you forget to turn the light off the first time you went?"

"Eh Greeno, I'm surprised you haven't told us all that you have also been to The Boulevard."

"That was in Paris."

"Was that the time you got plastered?"

It was a typical lunchtime slice of repartee. It was something that Wilkinson's draughtsmen were all good at, in addition to designing electrical control systems for operation in power stations, chemical plants, glass works, textile mills and more. But all this came to a halt as Jennifer walked into the office. She had spent the last two days at a factory up in the North East, fairly near to where she had once lived as a child.

She disappeared for a few minutes to warm up a pie in the microwave and as she sat down to eat it, Alan said: "Jennifer, did you know that while you were away and probably without your agreement or permission, the Government organised a by-election in Hull?"

She wiped all the crumbs from the pie into her waste paper basket, produced a custard tart out of her bag, and replied:

141

"Actually, it is a by-election in the Haltemprice and Howden constituency which is about 10 miles west of the city of Hull."

"And who is going to win?"

"I don't know. All that I do know is that neither the Labour Party nor the Liberal Party will."

"How do you know that?"

"Because I don't think that they are going to stand."

"Why not? Have they finally learned that voting solves nothing because the Government always wins?"

"So go on then, tell us. Sounds a bit unusual to me."

But before any more could be explained by Jennifer, Duffy appeared on the scene and nothing more was said about the Haltemprice by-election.

On the following Friday, Alan worked until lunchtime, went home for his lunch and spent the afternoon working in the back garden. Time passed quickly and around half past six they set off on the short trip to Knowsley Road to watch the Saints demolish Castleford 68–12. This time though they went on their own as their neighbours Phil and Janice were away for a week on holiday in Normandy where Janice had a relative.

They arrived in their usual spot quite early and looking around Alan saw a woman who he had not seen for quite a long time, standing there on her own.

"Hello there. Haven't seen you for quite a while. Where's your other half tonight?"

She smiled at him sadly, then pointed her index finger upwards and said: "He's up there with Joe Ball, Jimmy Stott, Alan Prescott, Duggie Greenall, Stan McCormick and all the rest of them."

"Oh, I am sorry. Had he been ill? I don't think that we have seen you at all, this season."

"He was very ill right at the end. All those years at Ravenhead did him. Emphysema it was. He coughed his way into his coffin. I'm glad he's gone. It wasn't a life for him, not right at the end."

As Alan began to offer his condolences, their conversation, was interrupted by the arrival of the Saints on to the field and the next time he noticed her, she was stood talking to another man who Alan had also not seen for ages. He was probably another fan too, one who could also remember Joe Ball, Jimmy Stott, Duggie Greenall, Alan Prescott, Stan McCormick and all the rest of them.

The incident had put him in quite a melancholy mood as Thelma drove them home.

"Do you know what? I can still remember the first time I ever met her husband. It was in the Cup in 1959 and we were away at Featherstone. I'd gone with a few lads from Sutton. That day there were three train loads went from Shaw Street station. There were eight of us in our carriage and he was with us. I think that was the first time that I had ever been to Yorkshire before and we got beat in the snow. After that I often used to see him on the terraces when we were at home. I didn't know that he worked at Ravenhead. In fact I hardly knew a thing about him, other than he was a red hot Saints fan. I didn't even know what his name was."

"How well can you remember your first game, Alan?"

He then proceeded to tell her again about his uncle Jack and how he had acted almost like a father to him. And it was because he had been a big Saints fan, that Knowsley Road was one of the first places his uncle had taken him on one of their days out. Then Alan asked her if she could remember anything about her first visit to watch the Saints.

Yes, she could remember it. It had been an evening game against Oldham and was the very first time she had ever watched any form of sport. She remembered being stood there with Alan and three of his mates along with their girlfriends. It was also the first time that she had been in company with such a friendly group of people, one that had immediately warmly welcomed her into their midst.

She also recounted an incident that had occurred within the first few minutes of that game. Oldham had brought a large number of supporters with them and quite a few were standing right behind them. One was a right bag of wind, calling out against every Saints player, the referee and the two touch judges all the time. As he shouted, he kept lurching forwards and bumping into Thelma and Dorothy the girlfriend of Alan's mate Geoff. One of the other Oldham fans pulled the guy back and then said to Thelma: "You're aw reet, luv. He's harmless. He just gets excited. He's as bad as this when he comes fishing with us."

From that game she also recalled an occasion early in the second half. The Saints second-rower Dick Huddart had found a gap in the Oldham defence and set off on one of his great runs, 30, 40, maybe even 50 yards. As he ran with everybody cheering him on, she was heard shouting: "Go on, go on, go on, go on."

She also remembered choosing her favourite player. It was Wilf Smith, the Saints stand-off and probably the smallest man on the field and probably not much bigger than she was.

On the following Saturday they took Joanna out with them for the day. They would have taken her brother Josh as well, but he was far too busy playing rugby. They drove first to Burtonwood and then Joanna's dad drove the three of them to Warrington Central station. It was the first time that Joanna had ever travelled on a train. Everywhere else she went, had always been in the car. At Lime Street Station, they caught the train that went under the River Mersey and on to the Wirral. Joanna was very frightened while they were underground and clung very tightly to Granma. But when the train came back into the open air, she was so relieved. She was even more relieved when Granma asked if she wanted to repeat the journey on the way back or go by boat. She chose the latter.

On Monday, Duffy came into the office to tell Alan that from the following Monday he would be away for the next two weeks in hospital. He outlined which jobs had to be finished and when. From what he said, it would appear there would be little for them to work on after the end of August, and even though Alan was no longer on the staff, Duffy was putting him in overall charge of the office. So it was lunchtime before any more conversations about what had happened the previous Thursday could be started.

It had been a busy morning, partly saddened by the news that Maria, the wife of one of the wiremen, had died as a result of an accident in Culcheth the previous day. But that would not have altered the tone of the first lunchtime discussion of the week, which somewhat surprisingly was started by Colin who said: "Did you see that David Davies won his seat back last Thursday, Jennifer?"

"I did see it, Colin but thanks for bringing it to my attention."

"And did you see how many candidates were standing?"

"There were 26 altogether. Among them were the Miss Great Britain Party, the Monster Raving Loony Party, the Church of the Militant Elvis Party, the Make Politicians History Party and a load of independents."

"You missed the Green Party out. They didn't do too badly. They came second and got over 1,700 votes."

"So how many were standing as Independents, then?"

"About 20."

"What were they all independent of? Each other?"

144

"Probably."

"Tell me Jennifer, is your little party still going?"

"If you mean The Anti Gap League, we are not a party yet, Cliff. Just a group, but we are full of hope and enthusiasm."

"And how are sales of your magazine going?"

"We printed 40 copies of our first issue and it sold out. We printed 60 copies of our second issue and that sold out. For this one we have done a print run of 100. What does that tell you?"

"It tells me there must be around 100 people in Ashurst who must have a lot more money than sense."

The words were spoken by John Carter, the great defender of everything that Tony Blair, Gordon Brown and New Labour did, and always wanting to disagree with whatever Jennifer might have to say. He had just walked into the office, wanting a print of a drawing that Alan had drawn some six months earlier. Nothing resulted from his comment though as John's arrival was soon followed by the appearance of their boss.

The following Thursday, not being required at work, Alan went up to see Rebecca. It seemed quite a long time since the two of them had been able to spend time together, without interruptions from the children. As she made a drink for them, he saw Neil's collections of CDs and among them was one featuring Alan's favourite singer, Jimmy Nail, which led to Rebecca asking:

"Who were your favourite singers and groups when you were growing up, Dad?"

"The first piece of music that I can ever remember liking was called *Greensleeves*. It was the signature tune for *Children's Hour*, a programme on the Home Service that we always had on at home at five 'o' clock, when we were just starting our tea. A bit later, I always listened to *Dick Barton Special Agent*. It had a great signature tune too although I have never been able to find out what it was called."

Rebecca knew that when he started to answer a question like this, he would go on to tell her other interesting tales from his past and so she said nothing but just let him carry on.

"When I first started at Wilkinson's, Bill Hayley and His Comets were my favourite band. A few of us in Chisnall Avenue even tried to get a skiffle group going, but none of us were the least bit musical. *Rock around the Clock* was my favourite track then. During the summer of 1962 and just before I met your mum, I was involved in that big campaign to stop Lord Beeching closing Ashurst station and the line up to Leigh. My favourite bit of music then was *Walk on by*, sung by Leroy Van Dyke. Four nights a week, I still remember it well, walking by loads of houses getting signatures for our petition."

"Why not five nights a week?"

"Night school."

"Were you a Beatles fan?"

"Yes, but I also used to like Gerry and The Pacemakers. Some of that group were draughtsmen, not that that made their music any better. The following summer I became a big fan of the French singer Johnny Halliday. The previous two summers during the Works Shutdown, I had gone hitch hiking on my own all round France. One year I even got into Spain but only for just long enough to have a meal and so be able to say that I had survived living under Franco's fascist regime.

"In 1963 I went hitch-hiking again but this time I took your mum with me. I remembered when we told Granny what we were going to do. I think it shocked her a little bit. I'm sure that her main concern was about where we would spend each night. So I told her that we would stay in youth hostels, me sleeping in the boys' side and your mum in the girls' side"

"And?"

"Except for the first couple of nights when we did stay in a youth hostel, we stayed in the same room together in a bar or small hotel. That was when I discovered that your mum did not snore when she was fast asleep."

"Oh you naughty thing, Dad."

"Rebecca, your mother was just as naughty as me, I was very pleased to discover."

"And did Granny ever find out what you had done?"

"I don't think she ever did. But what difference would it have made to anything and it certainly made it a very pleasant 15 days and 15 nights."

"I can also remember the time your mum was so ill, that first Christmas back in 1962. I called round on Boxing Day morning to see how she was and Granny told me that Doctor Jackson had just left and said that she would have to stay in bed for at least a week. I asked Granny if I could go up and see her. She said 'yes' and then as I walked away from her towards the stairs, she said: "'Leave the

146

bedroom door open. Just in case.'"

They both laughed at this comment and then Rebecca asked him to carry on with his favourite records over the years.

"*Stop in the name of love* sung by The Supremes was how I remember the time when me and your mum got married. *Have you seen her* sung by The Chi Lites coincided with the very first time that I saw you and Thin Lizzie's *The Boys Are Back In Town* coincided with Robert's arrival in town. *Everybody wants to rule the world* by Tears for Fears was Top of the Pops when Granny told us that we could move into her house as she was happy to go and live in the Greenfield.

"Then, when our union DATA was fighting the redundancies at Jarratt's, a few of us got arrested for picketing their factory. Top record for me then was *Big River* sung by Jimmy Nail. It included the words *"The Neptune was the last to go, I heard it on my radio and then they played the latest number one".*

"The Neptune was the last ship they must have built up there. Another great song of his is called *Blue Roses*. Whenever I hear two lines in that now, I always think of what life must have been like for your mum when she was growing up as a little kiddie in that home in Cardiff."

"Are you going to sing them for me?"

"No, but I'll just repeat them for you: '*You need more reassurance than a frightened orphan child, that I'm always going to want you and I'll always be beguiled.*' There are couple of other lines that always strike a chord with me in that song as well.

'*This nursery rhyme is corny. It's stranded out of time. But it's simple and it's honest and since when was that a crime.*'

"You can always tell a good tale Dad, though I think you sometimes slip things in that are not quite true."

"I bet you will never believe it if I told you that I was once the main suspect in the killing of a six month old baby."

"Never!"

"It was when we were on strike one day and picketing the Warrington Road gates. One morning, a police inspector appeared and asked to speak to whoever was in charge. We all thought he was going to arrest Len, the Office Committee Chairman, but it wasn't anything like that. It was because a baby off the Brunswick Estate had gone missing and the police were organising a massive man hunt for it and needed members of the public to help them.

147

What we had to do was line up in front of some waste land in Gillarsfield. There were about 50 of us and about the same number of police all in a long line. What we then had to do was walk two steps forward, stop, look on the ground around us and then walk another two steps forward and do the same. If you saw anything like a dummy or some clothing, you had to shout out and put your hand up.

After we had been doing this for a bit, I saw something that looked a bit like a doll in the long grass, right in front of me. I put my hand up and shouted out loudly and this inspector came straight over and told everybody else to step back. He took my name and address and said that I was now the main suspect, but that it was only a legal formality.

The next day I had to go to the inquest in Liverpool and state exactly what I had seen. And if you don't believe me, I've still got a copy of that day's *Liverpool Echo* which covered the case on the front page and it included my name in it."

"And did they ever find out what had happened to the baby?"

"Yes. It was the mother who had killed it, but for whatever reason I never knew and never really wanted to know."

"While we have got a bit of time to go down Memory Lane Dad, tell me about when you first saw my mum and what were your first impressions of her?"

"I can remember it very well. There was me and a couple of other lads in the Print Room one morning. I had my head down a drawing cabinet, trying to get a print that had fallen off the rail and as I did, I heard Big Joan say loudly: "No more swearing in here, you lads. We've got a lady working with us now."

"So I put my head round the cabinet and shouted out:

"Well she'll be the first lady they have had in here for a very long time."

"Then I looked at her and the first thing I saw was a young woman, a bit on the short side, with a nice face covered in freckles, her hair a right mess though and quite scruffily dressed. So I smiled at her and said: "Welcome to the Mad House."

"After that, I used to chat with her quite a lot, but she was so shy and never really said much. I quite liked her but around that time I was going out with a nurse from Knotty Ash who worked at Whiston Hospital. But we finished not long after. Well, we never really got started, what with her crazy shift system and her living

148

miles away in Diddyland.

A few days later it was Christmas Eve. I had lost my ticket to get into the dance at the Co-op Hall which was why I was stood on my own on the pavement outside, wondering what to do next. Then the number five bus pulled up right in front of me and as they changed drivers, I looked inside it and saw your mum sat there on her own. So I waved to her to get off and took her to Mario's coffee bar in Bridge Street for a hot drink.

It was then that I discovered that she had been brought up in a home in Cardiff, was lodging in Grasmere Avenue and was going to be on her own all over the Christmas holidays. So I invited her to spend the next day with all our family at Granny's. It must have been the first time that she had ever had a meal with a family. She was all right at first but then it all became a bit too much for her and she fell ill, stayed the night and then went down with pneumonia. Granny looked after her for the next few weeks, nursed her back to health and by the time she had recovered and was ready to go back to work, they had virtually adopted her and as they say, the rest is history."

"It certainly was."

"In fact it was a fine example of how a bad thing can often be turned into a good thing. Since then I have often wondered what might have happened to her if I had not lost my ticket to get into that dance or if she had caught an earlier bus or even was sitting upstairs on the same bus but that is something that none of us will ever know."

"That's right Dad. That's something that we'll never know and I wouldn't want to know either."

149

22. The lady from Sint-Jans-Molenbeek

It was raining heavily as Alan walked into The Volunteer for the draughtsmen's regular get together. This was both a talking shop and also an opportunity for anybody who needed some help or advice to get it from an old friend. In some cases, it was also a time when one of them would have his first laugh since the last time they had all been together. Never was the old saying that "You don't stop laughing because you grow old. You grow old because you stop laughing" found to be true.

It was certainly true for John Carr who lived with his Sunday school teacher wife Clare and their recently returned from the Bible Belt in America, daughter, Felicity, who saw the work of the Devil in just about every human being who lived in Astley.

As Alan walked into the bar, he saw Pete Mulholland talking to the manager Kevin. They went into the best room and sat down in the corner, with Pete saying that he thought the weather might put a few of them off. Also, of those who always turned up, one was currently in Whiston Hospital. Most of the others might appear or maybe not, as the weather was pretty bad outside.

Before Pete could say much more, Len Gamble, Ronnie Harper and Bernard Harrison stumbled into the room.

"Greeno, do you still believe in the existence of the Heavens?"

"Why."

"Because they have just opened up in Bridge Street."

"Why didn't you bring an umbrella with you?"

"Real men like me don't use umbrellas."

A few minutes later in walked Eric Hindley, dry as a bone and shaking his umbrella right in front of Bernard. Eric was a bit of a tough guy. He had played soccer for Dawson's Social Club and been sent off twice, rugby league with Helmsley Hornets and been sent off three times and had once wrestled with Shirley Crabtree in a club in Bolton and been carried off after five minutes.

"Eric, Bernard here reckons that real men don't use brollies."

"I don't use a brolly either."

"What's that in your hand?"

"It's a parapluie. I bought it in Paris last year."

"So what's on our agenda today lads, other than apologies, last month's minutes and the date of the next meeting?"

150

"We could discuss climate change."

"Why don't we discuss something interesting for a change?"

"Let's change the subject. I'm getting bored with all this."

"We could talk about things we once drew on a board."

"Greeno, why don't you tell us again how you managed to go to that cotton mill in Portugal six times in one year and it only had three A4 sheets for all its details?"

"I could tell you all about how I went to Argentina for a textile machinery exhibition and spent the best part of a week there lying on the beach."

"What about number 99?"

"Oh, not that one again. Who was the fitter on that job?"

"Billy Jones. Didn't realise that 99 on a cable marker looked the same as 66 upside down."

Then Pete asked if anybody had heard anything about the Bradford and Bingley Building Society being in trouble. Nobody had, but clearly in the present financial world, anything was possible and there was now no certainty that any of their pensions or mortgages were safe, no matter where they were deposited.

"Count me out if you are all going to start talking about economics. It's even worse than talking about politics. Everybody has got a computer at home. Every man and his dog has an opinion about everything that's going on in the world now and nobody can agree about anything, especially this Labour lot."

It was John Mather's first contribution and typical of him too. He just didn't like things being discussed about the real world. Strange really, since his son had a degree in Philosophy and his daughter a degree in Social Science. His attitude to life ran along the lines that if you didn't know about anything bad that was going on in the world, that would make it easier to enjoy life.

"What's wrong with folk knowing a lot more about the world in which they live, John? Let's face it, nearly all the newspapers in this country are owned by five multi-billionaires. You don't think they will ever tell the truth about anything that affects us, do you."

It was Len Gamble, whose views had changed greatly after his wife had died and he had discovered that her insurance policy had not paid out what he had been led to believe it would do.

"It's a funny old world with everybody having a computer at home" said Ken Platt. "Some people can make a living just buying and selling stuff on the internet and they don't even see what they have bought or sold. Just how do they do it?"

"What amazes me is how language has changed since the arrival of the computer."

It was the first thing that Bernard Harrison had said since they had all sat down. "Once upon a time memory was something that you lost with age, a programme was a TV show, an application was for a job, a keyboard was a piano, a web was a spider's home, a hard drive was a long trip, and if you had a three-and-a-half-inch floppy, you just kept quiet about it."

"I tell you what, Bernard. It is a lot easier for me to keep in touch with our lad with this internet. Once I had to wait until three or four things had happened to me before it was worth writing to him in Portsmouth and then half of it would be out of date by the time he received it. Now he knows as much about what is going on in St Helens than I do and I live there."

"How does he do that, Eric?"

"It's on a website called *St Helens Connect*. You can even go on it and find out what happened to some of the people you once went to school with. Well, that's what he tells me you can do."

Despite having nothing on any agenda, they still talked among themselves for well over two hours. Some of them considered it to be like a therapy session. Ronnie once said that the only time he ever enjoyed life was when he was with them, while Bernard was always coming up with smart one-liners to cheer up anybody who was missing all the banter and fun of being in a group at work.

Like when he said: "I remember when I first left home. My mother said to me, don't forget to write. I said to her, mother I am 22 years old, I've been reading and writing since I was five. Why do you think that just because I am going to work in London I might forget how to write?"

One thing that all of those present always did was to ask Alan how Thelma was. Many of them had known her since her early days at Wilkinson's and had probably felt quite sorry for her then, well at least until she had started going out with "Greeno".

On Friday afternoon they went into St Helens and the first place they visited was Wardleworths Bookshop in Westfield Street. As they walked in, they saw Barbara stood at the far end, talking to a man who looked vaguely familiar. Alan heard her say to him:

"These two are big Saints fans" and as they walked towards her, she asked:

152

"Have you two met Alex Service before?"

They hadn't and soon got talking, with Alex telling them that he and his colleague Denis Whittle were shortly bringing out a book about the history of Pilkington Recs. Alan told Alex that one of his workmates came from a family that had a relative who was on their committee in the 1930s. But it was now too late for any more information to be included as the final version of the book was now with the publisher in London.

On Saturday morning they went to watch the under-9s game between Gillarsfield Giants and Astley Roosters. For them, the main attraction was their grandson Josh, now developing quite a nice side-step, which he used three times to score his fourth hat-trick of the season. A nice group of parents were in attendance too, including three mothers and a woman who Thelma had not seen since they had both finished working at Wilkinson's.

On Monday, Alan told Cliff about the soon-to-be-published book on the history of the Recs. Cliff had grown up on Mulberry Avenue less than 10 minutes' walk from the Saints ground. Despite that, both his parents had little interest in rugby. However, one pair of grandparents lived down Windle City within sight of the Recs' old ground and it was from that side of his family that much of Cliff's knowledge of the game had come. His other grandparents had lived in Kirkland Street. But that grandfather had died on the Somme in 1916 and his grandmother never spoke about him.

Although Cliff had obviously never seen the Recs play before the Second World War, he still had a great interest in their history. He was also an occasional spectator at some of their big games. Two games that had stood out for him were both played at Knowsley Road and in each case had attracted a crowd of over 11,000 spectators to see them play top professional clubs.

The first one was in 1977 when the 'Reckreashun' almost beat Wigan in the Challenge Cup first round, losing in the end 10–4. The following year they came even closer, losing by one point to Castleford in a 23–22 thriller. Two years later he also remembered going to Borough Park in Blackpool to see them beat Dewsbury Celtic in the 1980 BARLA National Cup Final.

Sadly, he was also present on the occasion of the Rec's darkest hour at a game played at their original City Road ground in 1971. It was against their local rivals UGB, a game in which their captain, Jackie Pimblett, a glass cutter at Pilkington's by trade, sustained

153

severe spinal injuries that led to his death four days later in a Southport hospital, leaving a widow and two young sons.

The next night, with Alan facing defeat yet again on the chess board, they were interrupted by the arrival of their friend Ray. The main reason for his visit was to tell them about the funeral arrangements of Stan Battersby who had recently died at the ripe old age of 98.

'Batters' had been in charge of Wilkinson's Drawing Office when nearly 100 electrical, mechanical, sheet metal and jig and tool draughtsmen worked there along with six tracers and five checkers. He was a well-liked character, firm but fair, and always prepared to turn a blind eye to some of the stupid things that any of the younger draffies might have done, as Alan knew well.

It is often said that you can tell how well liked a person had been in life by the number of people that turned up for his or her funeral. Stan's funeral was held in St Austin's Catholic Church in Gillarsfield and to it had come over 100 former work mates, some of whom came from as far away as Preston and Coventry.

This was all in stark contrast a few years earlier to the funeral of their former Assistant Chief Draughtsman J. Arthur (*You can't do enough for a good firm*) Wood, commonly known as Lurch. At his funeral there had just been the three men who came with the hearse. Even the Vicar of St Luke's Church had turned up late.

Then Thelma asked Ray how Jeanne was readjusting to life back in Ashurst.

"Much of it is still all a great shock to her. I drove her all round Eccleston to where there were once just green fields. Now it's all houses. She used to live for a while near Cook's Farm at the bottom of Kiln Lane and that went a long time ago. She was shocked to see that Helena House in Baldwin Street and the market where her auntie used to have a stall, had gone as well as Knowsley Road School. She was pleased to see that the Saints ground was still standing there though I didn't have the heart to tell her that might be going soon."

"And how is she spending all her time having you and all your investigations to put up with?"

"Very well. A few weeks ago I took her round to meet my cousin Ann who lives up Hard Lane in St Helens and they clicked straightaway. Ann has really come out of her shell, since her husband died. She has even helped start a 'Save The NHS' group and Jeanne has joined it. They've got about a dozen members already and they are nearly all women, not that there's anything wrong with that. Far from it.

One funny thing about Jeanne though is that when she lived in Brisbane, she was regularly on the internet trying to find out what was going on in St Helens. Now that she is living here, she is regularly on the internet trying to find out what is going on in Brisbane. Makes me laugh, it does."

Then he said a very odd thing about the person who he was clearly now deeply attached to: "I have to say though that I have never met a more negative person in all my life than Jeanne."

"You surprise me saying that, Ray. From all of what you have said about her so far, I thought that you would have said the very opposite."

He laughed, in such a way that they knew that what he had just said was another one of his clever play on words.

"Before she went to Australia, she was a keen photographer. It was something that she shared with her dad. What the pair of them liked to do was to photograph buildings, factories or streets that were due for demolition both in Ashurst and in St Helens as well. Between them they accumulated a very large collection of photos, some which he had taken before the war or which he had acquired from various people and relatives over the years.

Luckily they had all been kept in boxes at her sister's house in Haydock. When I saw them all, I got this idea of putting the most interesting ones together in a book, and write short stories about them based on whatever I could find out from former residents or people who had relatives or neighbours who had once worked there if it was say a factory or a pit or a shop.

I mentioned this idea to a couple of my old mates and got them to ask around for any old photographs that any of their relatives might lend me. I've now got loads including some really old ones of Ashurst Station, the old Town Hall before it got burned down, Bold Power Station with its cooling towers half built, one of a funeral party setting off from a house in Seddon Street down Windle City in 1899 and quite a few of Pudding Bag too."

"Whatever is Pudding Bag" asked Thelma.

"It was the name of a district of Sutton that was close to St Helens Junction railway station. It was made up of about 50 houses in three streets built in a triangular shape. Around 200 people lived there until the Council knocked it down in the 1970s. They were nearly all people who worked on the railway or their relatives. I knew a lot about the place because my Auntie May lived there nearly all her life."

I have also discovered a website called *A History of Old Sutton.* It covers that area in great detail and have been on the St Helens Connect web site again to see if there any of its former residents still around. One old lady has already contacted me and invited me to go and see her if ever I am anywhere near where she now lives just outside Perth."

"What's the chance of you ever going up to Scotland, Ray."

"What's Scotland got to do with it? It's Perth in Western Australia where she lives now."

He then asked Alan if he could remember a former Wilkinson's apprentice by the name of Eric Liptrot.

"I do. He was a bit younger than me and lived at the back of the Wigan Arms up Nook End. After he came out of his time, he worked in the Copper Mill for a while and then he got a job with BICC at Prescot with their Overhead Lines Department. Sometime later I heard that he had gone working in the Middle East. Why?"

"I called in the Trades Club last week for a game of snooker with our Jack. I bought myself a pint looked round to see where he was and saw Eric sat at a table on his own in front of two nearly full pints. I sat down and chatted with him for a bit. He asked me if any of his old mates were still around town and was particularly pleased to hear that you were still with us. Then he told me that he reckons that you still owe him 10 bob plus interest from some apprentices' night out that you both once went on, at the Grafton down Liverpool in 1958.

Then, a very smart looking woman appears and sits next to him and starts drinking from one of the glasses. He introduced her, said that her name was Louise and they had met about six months earlier when he had been on holiday in Paris. Then he told me that she had been born in Stalingrad and had lived there until she was 10 years old.

Now, I can speak a little bit of Russian so I said a few words to her. To my amazement she said, in quite good English, that she could not speak Russian. Bit unusual her saying that, you would think."

"Knowing you there must be a catch in this one somewhere."

156

"There is. She's Belgian and a few miles west of the centre of Brussels there is a district called Stalingrad. Her family used to live there until her father died causing the rest of the family to move a few miles away to a place called Sint-Jans-Molenbeek."

"What's she like?

"A bit of a talented one, you might say. She can speak half a dozen languages, once worked for the French paper Le Figaro and also writes occasional articles for a Belgian English language newspaper."

Alan laughed and said: "After Brussels and Paris, I think she'll find life in Ashurst will be a bit of a culture shock for her. I wonder how long she'll last."

Their conversation was interrupted by a call from Cliff ringing from a sub-station in Bootle where he had spent the last two days. It was to tell Alan that he would have to be away from the office for another day because he needed more time to sort out what was now turning into quite a major problem. As Alan put the phone down, Thelma said to Ray: "What bearing will all this photography business have on your exposure of the evils of neo-liberalism in the world today then?"

"Not very much I would reckon, Thelma. Neo-liberalism only reared its ugly head in the 1970s. Most of these photos were taken years before then, some of them probably while Karl Marx was still in a library in London somewhere proof reading Das Kapital."

Then he turned back to Alan and said: "I've got a couple of photos that will definitely please you, Alan. They show the Saints team getting into a horse drawn wagon outside the Talbot in Duke Street, ready to go up to Knowsley Road for a match. No sign of the other team though. I bet that they made them walk it there and back. No wonder they always used to win when they played at home."

23. Marsha is belting at skipping

"Granma, can we do some talking?"

"Of course we can. Have you got something to tell me about your new school?"

"Yes. It's really nice. We are doing all sorts of interesting things and I've got a lot of new friends as well."

"What is your teacher's name?"

"It's Mrs Banner."

"Is she nice?"

"A little bit. She's not as nice as Mrs Foster though."

"You liked Mrs Foster a lot, didn't you?"

"Yes, I did. I'm going to write her a letter telling her how I am getting on after I've been there a few more days."

"Well, I am sure she will like that."

Then Granma asked if she stayed for her dinner every day.

"Yes."

"What's the food like?"

She pulled her face a bit and said: "It's all right but it's not as nice as what you or mummy make."

"Do you have to share a desk with anyone?"

"Yes. We all do."

"And who do you share with?"

"Marsha. She's my bezzie."

"Whatever is a bezzie?"

"It means she's my best friend."

"What's she like?"

"She's quite tall, she has a long ponytail and do you know what, her skin is brown all over. I think she must have been on her holidays somewhere."

"And what does she like to do?"

"She's belting at skipping. She just goes on and on all through play time."

"Do you like skipping?"

"Yes, but I am not as good as she is."

"And what else can you tell me about her?"

"Well, she talks a little bit funny."

Then she looked up into her grandmother's face and said: "I think that you talk a little bit funny too, Granma?"

"Do you mean that I talk a little bit different than your mummy and your daddy?"

Joanna nodded.

"I mean it's not funny, it's just different."

"That's because I grew up a long way from Ashurst. It was in a place called Wales. You knew all about that, didn't you?"

"Yes."

"Do you think Marsha sounds like me?"

"No. She doesn't sound like you and she doesn't sound like my mummy either, but she's nice."

"Good, that's the main thing."

It was Saturday morning and Joanna had just been dropped off by her mother before going into Warrington to do a bit of shopping. It was also the first time Joanna had seen her grandmother since she had started at her new school.

The next hour was then spent in the kitchen, with Joanna helping Granma make a cake. Then she decided to go upstairs and tell Little Ted about Marsha and all her new friends.

A few minutes later Rebecca came into the house from her trip into Warrington.

"Has she been telling you all about her new school, Mum?"

"Yes. She has and she seems to like it there."

"She does. As soon as she comes home she tells me all that they have done that day. Not sure how long that will last but she certainly seems to have got off to a good start. Much better than Josh ever did."

"She's told me quite a bit about her new friend too. From what she has said, it sounds to me as though Marsha comes from a South Asian background."

"What did she say?"

"She said her skin was brown all over and she talks in a funny way."

"I've met both Marsha and Kulvinder her mother, and as soon as either of them started to talk, I could tell that they were not from round here."

"Do they both sound a little bit like Peter Sellers, then?"

"No. They both sound a little bit like Peter Kay. Before they came here, they used to live in Blackburn."

"Well that's put me in my place."

"It certainly does. You'll be asking me next if her daddy drives a bus for Arriva."

"Does he?"

"No he doesn't. He works at Warrington Hospital."

"What is he, a porter?"

"Mum, you are really stereotyping today. Her daddy is actually a brain surgeon."

"Won't be much call for that in Warrington, I would think."

"Mother. Have you been drinking?"

"No, but I wouldn't mind one. What do you want? Tea or coffee?"

The next time they were together was the following Saturday morning. Rebecca was taking some of the clothes that she had bought the previous week, back to Warrington. As she and Joanna walked into the living room, they found Granma sat in front of a large pile of books on the big table.

"Hello, you two. If you wonder what I am doing sat here, I am having a big clear out. We are really short of books to sell in the shop and I'll never read most of these again, so I'm going to take some of them to the shop sometime next week."

Then she took one of those that she was keeping and said: "This one must be over 50 years old. I think I'll keep this and read it when I can find some time."

"What is it, Mum?"

"Teach yourself to speak Welsh."

"That will be too hard for me. I think I'll manage with basic English in Warrington this morning."

As Rebecca left the room, Joanna picked up the book and went and sat on Granma's lap.

"What is this book all about, Granma?"

"It's about the language that people speak in Wales. Do you want me to read some words to you?"

Joanna smiled and nodded.

"Un, dau, tri, pedwar, pump"

"What's that, Granma?"

"It's the numbers one, two three, four, five."

"Say it again!"

"Un, dau, tri, pedwar, pump."

Joanna tried to repeat the words but couldn't at first.

"Would you like to learn how to speak a little bit of Welsh?"

"Yes please."

"Well, let's do it secretly. Don't let your mummy or daddy know

160

and then when you have learned it a little bit, we can surprise them both. Do you agree?"

She did.

"Fy enw I yw Joanna Rigby"

"What's that?"

"My name is Joanna Rigby."

Then Thelma continued: "Yr wyf yn bum mlwyd oed."

"I am five years old."

And so they both began to learn to speak in Welsh with Joanna picking up the words quite quickly.

The following Saturday morning they were all together yet again, with Joanna having some news to tell Granma about Marsha. Over the previous weekend, her best friend had fallen down the stairs at home and now had her arm in plaster. On the Monday she was not in school and Mrs Banner had told all the class what had happened to her. She also asked Joanna if she would like to visit her and so after the last lesson, she walked out with Joanna to where all the parents were waiting and given Rebecca, the telephone number of Marsha's mother.

Later that evening, Rebecca rang Kulvinder and arranged to visit the next day after school. As soon as they arrived, Marsha took Joanna straight up to her bedroom. Kulvinder took Rebecca into the front room and so began a friendship between a Welsh/Lancashire lady and a Punjabi/Yorkshire lady although one with a broad East Lancashire accent. It turned out that Kulvinder had been born in the Airedale Hospital near Keighley in West Yorkshire, but when she was just six years old, her parents had moved across the border into Lancashire to live in Blackburn.

Joanna told Granma about what things were like in Marsha's bedroom. On the walls were pictures showing a village where Marsha's grandparents lived. But what was really strange was one particular sheet of paper in a large picture frame and on which were written what Joanna described as funny wiggly lines.

So Granma told her that the wiggly lines might be words written in a foreign language. Then she went on to explain that there were many languages in the world and there were many different ways of writing.

"Some languages are written like our language."

And with that, Granma wrote down the words "Ich bin funf", "J'ai cinq ans", and "Yr wyf pump" then explained that the first one was the German for "I am five", the second one was French for "I am five" and the third one was Welsh for "I am five".

"Do some more" said Joanna keenly and so Granma wrote: "Ja", "Oui" and "Le"

"That is the German, French and Welsh for the word yes."

"Do some more."

So Granma had proceeded to write down "Danke", "Merci" and "Diolch" and then explained what they all meant.

Knowing just how clever Granma was, Joanna then asked her to write something in that wiggly lines language that she had seen in Marsha's bedroom.

"I don't think that I can do that, Joanna but I can say a few words in that language. Would you like me to do that?"

"Yes please."

"Pinkily, pankily, ponkily, bum, bum, dadida, dadida, di da."

And then the big tickling session began as was often the case when the two were sat there together.

Later that evening Thelma told Alan about her and Joanna's excursion into the study of foreign languages. Then she asked him how many languages he could speak although he had probably told her more than once before.

"My best language is French but I can also get by in German, a bit less in Italian and I know a little bit of Polish."

This led on to him telling her about when he had been on holiday in Poland and had visited the former concentration camp at Auschwitz. He was in the main exhibition hall and had bumped into an old man, leaning on a walking stick. He apologised using the Polish word that he knew for sorry. The old man replied, but Alan could not understand. So he had said to him in Polish: "I am from England". The old man said 'gde' which means where, with Alan replying "Pomiedzy Liverpool i Manchester".

The man rolled up his shirt sleeve to reveal a number tattooed on his arm, then spoke to the woman who was with him. She took a piece of paper out of her handbag and gave him a pencil and then started to talk to Alan in Polish. He could not understand what she was saying and so he said "Parlez vous Francais", then "Parlo Italiano" and then he had wondered whether he should utter the words "Sprechen Sie Deutsch" in that terrible place.

Ironically she could speak enough German to tell Alan that he was her uncle and had spent time here during the war and what he

162

had written badly were details of his brother who had gone to live in Manchester in 1937 and who he had never seen since. It was almost impossible for Alan to read the name or the area where the man must have once lived. It looked much like Milas Pluttin, by which he probably meant Miles Platting.

Then the old man had shuffled away, probably full of emotion because of what he had once suffered there. The woman said that this was because it was the first time he had been in the place since being liberated by the Russians at the end of the war. Then she had taken hold of her uncle's arm and walked him away.

"And how much Polish can you speak?"

"Probably no more than a dozen words, all the important ones though like yes, no, where, when, what, how, one, two, three, how much is it, I am English and whose pies are they?"

After tea they both felt like spending the evening in the Ring o' Bells. When they arrived there, they found Mr and Mrs Winstanley and Mr and Mrs Liptrot sat there along with another former neighbour Dennis Cameron. At the time of his 21st birthday he must have easily weighed over 14 stone but approaching 50 now, he looked more like 17 stone, possibly even more.

Mrs Liptrot knew Dennis well because he used to live next door to her. When she saw him go to the bar and return holding a pint in one hand and another large pie in the other, she asked: "Have you not had any tea tonight, Dennis?"

He looked at her in amazement and said that he had. Why did she want to know?

"If your dear old mother was still with us, you know what she would say to you seeing how overweight you are. Don't eat between meals and for heaven's sake get some exercise. You are carrying far too much weight for your own good and I say all that because your mother was a very good friend of mine."

"Thank you for those kind words Mrs Liptrot, but to anybody who thinks exercise is good for you, just consider this.

"A whale swims all day, eats only fish, drinks only water and yet it is very, very fat. A rabbit runs and hops all day long and only lives for 15 years at the most. A tortoise does not run or hop, does next to nothing all day long yet can live for over 100 years. And yet people tell me to get some exercise. I don't think so."

He then looked at his watch, saw that it was quarter to nine and said there was some darts that he wanted to watch on the television

163

starting in 10 minutes time so he was going to leave now, having just drunk his pint in three large gulps.

"Did you say the darts starts at nine o'clock?" said Alan. "Well you'll never get back to your house in 10 minutes.

"I will" said Dennis. "I've just booked a taxi. Toodoloo."

A few minutes later Mr Winstanley read out the headlines in the *Evening Post*. It was something along the lines of the need for all the countries in Western Europe to integrate their economies in order to survive in difficult world economic times. Then he went on to mouth his usual Little Englander philosophy by saying: "I'm bloody fed up with all this Common Market business. This country can easily look after itself. We can make what we want, we can keep the pound and we can leave the rest of Europe to do whatever it wants to do as well. And let us just see who comes out on top and it won't be them bloody Frenchies or them lazy Ities."

"Frank, your car is German, your pizza is Italian, your coffee is Brazilian, your tea and your shirt comes from India and the oil in your car is from Saudi Arabia. Your electronics are Chinese, your numbers Arabic, your letters are Latin and your vodka is Russian so what do you think about all that?"

Before Frank could say anything, Alan continued: "My great grandmother came from Wales and so does my wife and her father was from Greece. Where would we all be now if they hadn't come to live here?"

Then much to their surprise Frank's wife chipped in and said: "You might be surprised to know that his grandparents came from Southern Ireland, our eldest daughter now lives in the south of Spain with her husband who has an Italian mother and a French father."

She went on to say that the trouble with him was that he thought that everything that he read in the *Daily Mail* was true. Then as she put her hand on his knee she said: "I still love him after all these years and I always will do. But it isn't for his intellect or his table manners or his attitude to anybody who wasn't born in Lancashire."

24. He's in St Helens Hospital

After she parked the car outside the house, Rebecca said: "No sign of the car, Joanna. Grandad must be at work again."

She walked up the steps and unlocked the front door to let Joanna rush into the house as she always did. She went back to collect her shopping bag and saw Thelma's next door neighbour Janice walking towards her. As they started talking, Joanna came rushing out of the house and said loudly.

"Mummy, come quickly. There's something wrong with Granma. She's in the kitchen with her coat on and she's crying. I think she must be poorly. Come quickly."

She rushed back into the house, followed by Rebecca and Janice and then as the first one into the kitchen, she had stood there and pointed at her grandmother, almost as though Rebecca might not know which one was her mother. Quite humorous really, at a time of possible great sadness.

"Mum, what's up. Have you hurt yourself or are you ill or has something happened to Grandad?"

Granma smiled, wiped the tears from her cheeks and said: "Hallo, you lot. There's no need to worry about me. I was just thinking about Granny. It's her special day today, you see. Its 25 years since she left us and I was just thinking about her, how much I loved her and how much I still miss talking to her."

"And why have you got your coat on. Where are you going?"

"If you look on the table in the living room, you'll see a big bunch of daffodils. They were her favourite flowers and I am going to take them up to the cemetery. I always do on this day."

"How were you going to get there? You weren't going to walk it in this weather, were you?"

Before her mother could reply, Rebecca said that she would take her up in the car. Then Janice realised that it might be the first time Joanna had ever been to a cemetery and perhaps that might upset her. So she suggested that Joanna stayed with her as she had something she wanted to show her. It was probably something to do with her paintings and it was.

An hour later, Alan walked into the house. He had been at work all day and it was where he and all the rest of the Drawing Office had been given some bad, though not unexpected news. The head office in Amsterdam had finally decided to close down all their operations in the UK and France although no dates had been given.

Alan had always enjoyed his time working there. The main reason was because of the number of great characters he had got to know. His second reason was because he had always enjoyed designing electrical control systems in a wide range of industries. And thirdly he had also enjoyed going abroad on jobs and meeting people from right across Europe and even further afield.

He thought he might have been sad, but he wasn't. He also suspected that he would probably get called back again to deal with problems on machinery that had already been installed but needed modification. But he could not find enough energy or enthusiasm to go back there at the moment and so later that evening he suggested to Thelma that it might be a good idea to go away for a few days. This would also make it a lot easier for Robert and Megan to move in temporally, while their house was being rewired and then decorated.

They set off the following morning with Thelma driving, after having rung Megan to tell her what they had planned for the next few days. They headed towards the East Lancs Road, then joined the M6 at Junction 23 and headed north. They soon approached Junction 25 and with a sign post indicating the road to Wigan.

"Should we turn off here and get some pies to eat on the way?"

"No, just carry on."

Thelma actually didn't have a clue where they were heading but it wouldn't be the first time he had done something like this. She remembered when he had taken her to Rugely Power Station in Staffordshire. There he had spent an hour in a meeting, returned to the car and continued to drive further south all the way down to Didcot Power Station where he had delivered a box of Swedish electronic meters. After that it was on to South Wales and where the following morning he had spent time at Aberthaw Power Station. And on that particularly trip, they had stopped for their lunch in the small town of Tonyrefail.

She also knew that he always enjoyed his trips up to Blyth Power Station on the Northumbrian Coast. Perhaps that was where they were heading today although she was sure he had recently told her that it had been demolished and so that was not their destination. They turned off the M6 at Junction 37 and headed west towards the Cumbrian coast. Maybe we are going to Whitehaven or

Workington, she thought. But again she was wrong when as they approached the town of Grasmere, he told her to turn into the car park of a small hotel. It was to be the place that they would stay for the next two nights.

"We had a school trip here in 1955. There were two things that I particularly remember about it. One was visiting William Wordsworth's cottage and the other was climbing up Helvellen. I've never been back since, but have always wanted to so I thought this could be a nice little trip for us."

The following morning they spent an hour in the cottage before setting off on the next stage of this great mystery tour. An hour later they were stood outside Derwent Park, the home of the Workington Town rugby league club, one that Alan had never visited before, now another one to cross off his list. Then they drove down to Silloth where he had once spent a weekend. It was where an old mate from Gillarsfield had relatives and where he and Alan had stayed one Saturday night before going the short distance to the Recreation Ground, where Whitehaven played.

The following night they spent in Fleetwood. There was no rugby connection though, just a place where Alan had once attended a weekend school organised by the Draughtsmen's Union in 1964. Then back home and time to sit back and plan what to do next.

He was now spending more and more of his time on his computer. Every morning he would check his E-Mails, then visit the Red Vee, rlfans.com, Total RL.com and other interesting websites. He was also spending a lot more time working on his family tree.

Every now and again he would hear of an old school pal or former apprentice who had died or maybe a former neighbour from Chisnall Avenue. Often in *League Weekly* or *League Express* he would read of the death of a former player. Sometimes that player might be younger than he was. Sometimes it was a player that he knew and on odd occasions, one who was also a friend.

Thelma still worked as a volunteer a couple of mornings a week in the local Oxfam shop. She was five years younger than Alan, a bit on the short side and still had a face covered with freckles. Once she had hated those so called 'kisses from the sun', now it didn't worry her. And she loved it when Joanna would sit on her lap and try to count them all but never seemed to get much past 20, before throwing her hands in the air and giving up.

Then right out of the blue, Alan had a phone call from an old friend. He hadn't intended to go out that evening but Liam convinced him that he should do and so they agreed to meet in the *Ring o' Bells* at eight. He told Thelma he would be back in time for the *Ten o'clock News*. He wasn't and neither was he back an hour later. Finally there was a knock on the front door. It was a policeman with the news that Mr Greenall was in St Helens Hospital and had been badly injured, though as yet nobody knew why and how.

The car was outside the house so clearly he had walked to the pub, but what had happened after that? She thought he had the keys with him so she dashed next door and asked Janice to drive her to the hospital. In less than 15 minutes she was there and a further 20 minutes passed before she was taken to a ward of four beds. There were bandages all round his head, blood on the blankets, his eyes shut and his dishevelled clothes strewn over all a chair. All the nurse could tell her was that he had suffered injuries to his head and face and had not yet regained consciousness. They did not yet know the full extent of his injuries and he was being monitored closely every 15 minutes.

She sat there numbed. She found it so hard to take it all in. She remembered the last time that she had seen him in a hospital bed. It was five years earlier after he had been hit by a piece of wood sticking out of the window of a van driving past Lindsay's pie shop on Mersey Street. He had also had a few minor injuries over the years as well and once broke his arm playing rugby at Clock Face, but he had always grinned and told her that he was a tough Lancashire lad and not to worry about him. But now he wasn't even able to speak. Maybe he would never speak to her again.

No one as yet, was quite sure just how serious his injuries were or maybe they had told her and it just hadn't gone in. Maybe he would recover but not completely, maybe spending the rest of his life in a bed or a wheelchair and needing continuous care. Maybe it would not be that bad, just no longer able to go out of the house or take her to Knowsley Road again to watch his beloved Saints. Would she ever go there on her own or maybe just with Phil and Janice? Maybe the last game she would ever watch would now be the previous Saturday when they had seen their team beaten by Leeds at Old Trafford in the Super League Grand Final. Would she ever want to go there again?

She held his hand. It was still warm. She could feel his pulse so she knew that he was still alive, but maybe only just and for how much longer, who could be sure. Because of the seriousness of his condition, there were curtains all round the bed. Every now and again they were parted and a head peeped through them. But they had nothing to say, no hope to give and with only a small amount of time before they had to go and treat someone else, someone who almost certainly would still be there in the morning.

She rang Rebecca on her mobile. Her daughter drove straight over and around one o'clock she took her mother back to Burtonwood. Spending the night there would be a lot better than spending the night sat on that hardback chair by his bed and better than going home and being there all alone. Perhaps the worst thing about staying at Rebecca's house though, was that the whole thing would seriously upset Joanna. She loved Grandad. She was always telling everybody how funny he was. Maybe that part of her life would now be coming to an end. It would surely have been a lot worse for Joanna though, if it had been Granma who was now lying in that hospital bed.

First thing the following morning, they rang to see how he was but all they were told was that he was stable and being continually monitored. After they had eaten their breakfast, Thelma asked Joanna if she would like her to walk with her to school. At the school gates, Joanna pushed up her face for a kiss and said some words she had once said to Granma a few months earlier. It was even more poignant now than it had been then.

"I'll always be your friend, Granma. I'll always look after you."

Thelma stroked her on the head, told her to have a nice day and then watched her trudge across the school playground. Normally Joanna would have rushed to join all the other girls in her class who were stood around at the far end near to the canteen. But not today. It brought tears to Thelma's eyes just watching her little granddaughter walking with her head facing down so slowly and sadly. Then Thelma slowly went back to Rebecca's house. As she approached it, she saw her daughter locking the front door.

"Mum, I've just had a phone call from the hospital. We've got to go there straight away. Come on. Get in the car."

"Why? What's happened? Has he..., has he.....?"

Thelma just could not manage to finish her question. Just a couple of words would have been enough for that. Words possibly like died, or passed away, or left us, or stopped breathing, all sprung to mind. And at this moment of utter grief for her and for Rebecca

169

too but perhaps most importantly for Joanna, who would miss silly old Grandad ever so much.

"A nurse has rung and said he's just sat up in bed and asked if he could have two Weetabix and a banana for his breakfast."

Soon they were walking through the main doors of the hospital. On the one hand they were relieved to hear that not only was he still alive, but had been able to sit up and ask for food. But maybe it might just have been somebody else and the nurse had made a mistake and so they felt it was that, as they entered his ward and seen the curtains still round his bed. One was partly open and they could see a doctor and a nurse bending over whoever was in that bed. Had there been a sudden relapse, had he taken a turn for the worse, were they too late. How cruel would that be?

"Mrs Greenall."

The words were spoken loudly by a tall nurse with a very sad face walking towards them from the other side of the room.

"We've had to move Mr Greenall."

Move him to where, the morgue maybe!

"He's in Ward Seven. I'll take you there. It's only next door."

There he was, with bandages wrapped around his head and covering his face on one side.

He was clearly not his usual self, but at least he was still alive. As he opened his mouth to speak slowly to them, they saw he had lost one of his front teeth. Bizarrely, he had mentioned to her a couple of days ago that he would soon have to visit the dentist as one of his teeth probably needed pulling out. And now it looked as though it might have been knocked out but by who.

His first few words though were proof that he was not that far from being his usual self.

"What kept you both? Was there summat good on Breakfast TV?"

And before long, another one of his favourite questions.

"Did you remember to lock the front door?"

They stayed with him for over an hour. He still seemed dazed, but was clearly well enough to have been moved into a general ward. Thelma and Rebecca then left and went into St Helens to do a bit of shopping. They visited Wardleworths Bookshop where Rebecca bought a couple of books for him. Barbara, the manager of the shop, on learning of his accident and knowing him fairly well, made the comment that what they had chosen, would cheer him up no end. Not everybody in Ashurst though, would enjoy reading *A history of the slag heaps of South Lancashire* or *The forgotten railway stations of St Helens, Widnes and Wigan.*

They had their lunch in the Almond in Barrow Street and then drove back home and were just in time to collect Joanna. Standing outside the school gates they watched all the other children running across the playground to their parents or whoever was collecting them. Among the last to appear though was Joanna holding the hand of her friend Marsha. She trudged along, face looking down at the ground just like she had done earlier that morning. It was Marsha who saw Joanna's mother and grandmother first. She said something to Joanna who looked up and saw them waving to her and looking very happy. Straight away the two girls began to run towards the gates.

"Is Grandad all right? Is he coming home soon? Can we go and see him?"

Marsha's mother Kulvinder walked over and of course did not know what had happened. Then Mrs Banner, appeared, holding Joanna's pencil case. Joanna had just left it on her desk. Mrs Banner went on to say how sorry she and all the children in her class had been to hear about what had happened. She was so pleased then to be told how it looked as though Grandad was going to be all right. And by now Joanna was telling all her friends the good news.

They bought their evening meal from the chip shop and as soon as they had eaten it, Joanna said that she was going to make a *Get Well Soon* card for Grandad. But it was going to be a few more days before she or Josh would be able to see him. But he did speak to them on his mobile every evening before they went to bed and tell them that he was slowly getting better and not to worry about him.

171

25. The CID are now involved

They kept him in hospital for a week until they were sure he was well enough to leave. His first visitor was a man from Ashurst CID, but Alan could tell him little about the whole affair. All he knew was that he had been in the pub with Liam for about 20 minutes when a man, who he had never seen before, had taken Liam to one side and soon after, Liam told him that he had something urgent to do and left. He finished his drink and walked out of the pub, went through Victoria Park and heard some men arguing among themselves near to the old bandstand. It must have been them who had attacked him because the next thing he could remember was being lifted into the back of an ambulance.

"Who were these men? Had you upset anybody in the pub? Have you been in any bother with any of your neighbours or people at work recently? Do you owe anybody any money? Who else was in the pub? Who was the man that your friend Liam went off with? What's Liam's surname and what's his address?"

These were some of the questions the police asked Alan the following day but all he could tell them of his attackers was, that by their accents, he guessed they probably came from somewhere north of Bolton, probably Blackburn or Burnley way. It must surely have been a case of mistaken identity.

Soon after, his visitors began to appear, Thelma, Rebecca and Neil, Phil and Janice, Cliff and Pete Mulholland as well as a few former workmates, but not Joanna or Josh. Granma thought a visit to the hospital would not be a good idea for ones so young.

On the morning of his release, he chatted with a lad from Parr who might have to lose his leg, following a motor bike accident at Carr Mill. It made him realise that his own injury was almost insignificant. Then in walked Rebecca to take him home.

As they stopped outside the house, she told him that they were going to play a trick on Joanna. She wrapped a bandage over the plaster on his head and all round his face. Then as he stepped onto the pavement, a neighbour walked past. Alan knew before the hour was out, the news of his return would be spread far and wide. As they walked into the living room, he saw Joanna sat there, holding a large '*Welcome Home Grandad*' card but with bandages on both her arms, her legs and over most of her face too. And she kept repeating the words.

"Oh dear. Oh dear. Oh woe is me. I am proper poorly."

He knew straight away it was a bit of a joke so quite happily, he went along with it: "Where's Joanna? Where is she? You said she would be here. Has she gone to school?"

"I'm here Grandad. Here."

"I can't see her anywhere. Granma, where is she?"

As Rebecca helped him sit down, Thelma could see that Joanna was clearly frightened by all his bandages, so she immediately began to unwrap them from around his face, Soon all that could be seen on Grandad's head was a large plaster and that one side of his face was black and bruised.

Then Rebecca proceeded to remove all Joanna's bandages. Doing all this had reduced the shock she might have felt if she had immediately seen the scar on Grandad's head, his black eye, his missing tooth and all the bruising on his cheek bone.

As they prepared to leave Robert and Megan arrived and by half past nine Alan was exhausted but still keen to watch the *Ten o'clock News.* The main item on it was about how the Government had bailed out several banks. An economist, being interviewed on *Newsnight* had also said that people in Britain would never quite appreciate just how close the country had come to a total collapse of its whole banking system.

The following morning, after breakfast, Thelma told him to remain seated at the table while she told him that she had worked out his recovery programme.

"These are the things that you will not be doing. Helping next door move any furniture, gardening and nipping off to meet all your old workmates. No doubt half of them will come here anyway. No washing up or using the hoover, not that you ever do. The doctor wants you to rest and I will make sure that you do just that. You can go on your computer for no more than an hour every day, you can play chess and scrabble with me and you can spend time reading some of those books you have been threatening to read ever since I've known you."

"Yes, boss."

"Yes, I am the boss and to make sure you do what I want you to do, I have chosen three books for you to start off with. You have probably read all your rugby league books, so these are a bit different and might just broaden your vision as well."

173

"The first one is called *St Helens – An Industrial Town*. It's a collection of interviews with local people in the Thirties. The second is *Bloody Foreigners* and tells how the population of Britain has developed over the years. And since you keep coming up with that old Chinese saying "A journey of 10,000 Li begins with the first step", the third one is called *Red Star Over China*. It was written by Edgar Snow and is an account of an 8,000 mile march by the Chinese Red Army in the 1930s.

"You can chose what order that you want to read them in, but I'll be wanting to know each day what you have read. OK?"

Her first choice was of great local interest because St Helens and Ashurst were no more than five miles apart. He had often said to her that he wished he knew more about the history of the British Isles, having read some of *Bloody Foreigners* and found it very interesting. Now he was under orders to read it all. He had always had an interest in China and was frequently heard applying some of Chairman Mao's famous sayings to what was happening in what he liked to call the Worker's Democratic Republic of Ashurst.

"Jennifer has also left a copy of an article for the next issue of *The Gap*. I think there is something wrong in it so one of your tasks is to discover what I think it is."

At that point there was a knock on the front door. It was Janice and Phil. As soon as they walked into the room, Alan said:

"I'm not moving that bloody sideboard again."

"Don't worry Alan, it can wait until the weekend."

"That's all right as long as it's not one of this year's weekends."

"Actually I've brought a painting that I have done for you. I have called it *A Flash of Light*. It's inspired by a photograph of Pennington Flash that I took last week when we were in Leigh."

"Are you allowed to drink alcohol, Alan?"

"Why, have you brought some with you, Phil?"

"No, but I know where there is some quite near."

"Don't bother. I'd better leave it for a couple of years."

The following morning after Thelma had gone out shopping, he looked at what she had written on the sheet of paper she had left on the table. It said: "Read for half an hour. Put the casserole in the oven at 11.30. Ring Rebecca and Geoff Platt after 11."

He then decided to see if his memory had been affected, by writing the names of the children that had been in his final class at Lane Head Junior School. Soon he had the names of 13 boys and

174

eight girls. Not too bad for something that went back nearly 60 years. Nothing wrong with that part of his brain that was linked to memory, then.

Astbury: Took over his Dad's joinery business in Billinge

Ashcroft: Worked for the NCB at Southport Edge

Barrow: Joined the Royal Navy when he was 19

Barton: Went to live in Florida

Clarke: Held a high level position in the Civil Service in London

Critchley: A chemical engineer for ICI in Widnes

Davies: Played the drum in the Salvation Army band

Higham: A tool maker at Mather's Foundry

Mellor: Worked all his life in Wilkinson's Machine Shop.

Morris: Died of a heart attack at the age of 40

Platt: Worked as an electrician with NORWEB

Rhoden: Worked on a farm at Rainford

Winstanley: Worked as an electrician with MANWEB

Then he proceeded to write down the names of all the girls that he could remember:

Bridges: Worked in Germany as a seamstress for 11 years

Brown: A Sunday school teacher and a good tennis player.

Delaney: Secretary of Ashurst Young Socialists 1963 to 1965.

Jaundrill: Worked in the family greengrocers' shop in Hemsley.

Johnson: Owned a chip shop in New Brighton

Mills: Heavily involved in Green issues in New Zealand

Parry: Worked in the Wages Office in St Helens Town Hall

Prescott: Had a long pony tail and now lived in Rainford

As he wrote the last name down, the phone rang. It was Barry Littler now living back in Billinge. He had been on holiday and had not heard about what had happened while he had been away. The reason for his call was to tell Alan that Stan Middlehurst had died. Three years ago Stan had come back to live in St Helens after having some years earlier moved to Eastbourne on the South Coast to be near to where his daughter now lived.

As he put the phone down, Alan remembered one of Stan's main reasons for coming back to his home town. It was to watch the Saints again, something that he had greatly missed while living far away. Well, Stan had been well entertained by what the Red Vee had done on the field since his return. Three good years they had been. They had won the Challenge Cup, topped the Super League table and played in the Grand Final for each of those three years. They had also been chosen as the BBC Sports Personality Team of the Year in 2006 and seen Paul Wellens in 2006, James Roby in 2007 and James Graham in 2008 win the Man-of-Steel Award for player-of-the-year as well.

As he sat there, the pain in his head began throbbing. This time it was much worse than before. He didn't know whether to go and look for some painkillers or just wait until it went away. The chair was so comfortable, one that he had enjoyed sitting in for years. It had always been called Granddad's Chair even as far back as 1965 when his own grandfather had retired and he and Granny had splashed out and bought some new furniture and a black and white television set.

Then the door swung open and in walked Thelma carrying two large shopping bags. She put them down on the floor, took her coat off, hung it up under the stairs and, as she did, she said: "I saw Ken Rainford in ASDA this morning. He sends you his regards and said he'll be calling round to see you for a game of dommys if you are up to it.

"Oh great" said Alan, in a very disinterested way.

"He also told me what he has just heard about what both Labour and Tory governments have been doing with the miners' pension fund. They would appear to have been robbing it blind for years but he has only just heard about it from one of his old mates in Unite."

She took the bags into the kitchen, came back into the living room and as she sat down, she continued: "I met Maureen in Taylor's as well. Their Janet told her last night that a firm from Derbyshire has just been given a contract to deliver 90 panels of precast concrete for that sculpture they are going to build at Sutton Manor."

Normally Alan would have listened keenly to whatever she said about who she had met and what she learned from them but not today and she could tell it.

"Are you all right, Alan? You don't look so good."

"Have we got any Paracetamols anywhere? This pain in my head, it's killing me!"

Braver than all the rest

A mother fights for her son

Philip Howard

Dave and Sarah Burgess are devastated when their young son Karl is found to have muscular dystrophy. Then another tragedy hits the family hard. But the family are committed to do the best they can for Karl, who has a passion for rugby league. Based in Castleton, a Yorkshire town near the border with Lancashire, Karl's determination to get the most out of life, despite his disability, inspires those around him, in particular Chris Anderton, one of the Castleton Rugby League Club players, who is coming to the end of his career in the game. A moving novel of family life and rugby league.

Published in 2010 at £9.95, special offer £7.00 post free in UK direct from London League Publications Ltd. Credit card orders via www.llpshop.co.uk , orders by cheque to LLP, PO Box 65784, London NW2 9NS Also available as an E-Book for Kindle readers on Amazon.

The Glory and the Dream is a great rugby league novel. It tells the story of a young boy's rite of passage. It is full of rich characters, and is played out against a backdrop of social upheaval in the austere post-war years of rationing and shortages. But it was a time when communities pulled together. Walking days, royal visits, Sunday School outings to the seaside and communal bonfire nights were annual highlights. It was a time when youngsters had to make their own entertainment, including

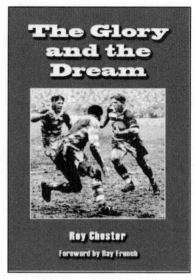

playing rugby league. It is about Johnny Gregson, the young star of the Garton rugby league team, whose dream is to follow his dad's success in the sport. Johnny lives with his mother in Four Locks, a poor working class area in a grimy northern town. His father died in the Second World War. The story starts in 1945, when Johnny is aged 10. It follows his rise from junior rugby league through playing rugby union as a schoolboy to turning professional with Garton.

Johnny faces challenges at every turn, including when he wins a scholarship to a local public school and is labelled as a 'slum kid' by the class bully. His prowess at rugby helps him deal with this boy. Also, at the tender age of 16, he meets a young woman who becomes very important to him. This is a story about sport, romance and working class life. It includes many humorous incidents, insights and even tragedy in a young man's development.

Published in March 2014 at £9.95. Order for **just £5.00 post free in the UK** from www.llpshop.co.uk or from London League Publications Ltd, PO Box 65784, London NW2 9NS. Also available on Amazon.co.uk
Also available as an E-Book for Kindle from Amazon.